TREY ELLIS'S

PLATITUDES

PLATITUDES

TREY ELLIS

VINTAGE
CONTEMPORARIES

VINTAGE BOOKS
A DIVISION OF RANDOM HOUSE
NEW YORK

Fiction
Ellis

A VINTAGE ORIGINAL, July 1988
FIRST EDITION

Library of Congress Cataloging-in-Publication Data
Ellis, Trey.
  Platitudes.
  (Vintage contemporaries)
  "A Vintage original"—T.p. verso.
  I. Title.
PS3555.L617P57 1988   813'.54   87-40109
ISBN 0-394-75439-5 (pbk.)

Text photos by Lorna Simpson

Designed by Ann Gold
Manufactured in the United States of America

10 9 8 7 6 5 4

PLATITUDES

Brian O'Nolan[1] once wrote that the modern novel should be largely a work of reference.[2]

That sounds very well, gentlemen, said Lamont, very well indeed in my humble opinion. It's the sort of queer stuff they look for in a story these days. Do you know?

Oh, we'll make a good job of this yarn yet.[3]

---

1. A.K.A. Flann O'Brien and Myles na gCopaleen.

2. "The entire corpus of existing literature should be regarded as a limbo from which discerning authors could draw their characters as required, creating only when they failed to find a suitable existing puppet. *The modern novel should be largely a work of reference.* Most authors spend their time saying what has been said before—usually said much better. A wealth of references to existing works would acquaint the reader instantaneously with the nature of each character, would obviate tiresome explanations and would effectively preclude mountebanks, upstarts, thimbleriggers and persons of inferior education from an understanding of contemporary literature. Conclusion of explanation." (italics mine) (*At Swim-Two-Birds*, Flann O'Brien, New York: Plume, 1966, p. 33)

3. Ibid., p. 245.

1

The digital alarm clock rolls little 7, 0, and 0 cards, white on black, over the 6, the 5, and the 9.

WAAAA—

Off. Waffle-colored fingers have crawled from under both the regular and the fitted sheets, which have been detached from the bed, twisting around his waist, between his legs. Earle's finger has pressed the white clock button in to free it to poke farther out. Light pours through the apartment window over the large schefflera leaves; it filters past the P38 Mustang and the four-stage Estes Saturn 5 rocket (one nose-diving, the other rising, but both from monofilament fishing line lashed to the curtain rod, and both stream red-dyed cotton-ball flames). Quivering shadows dapple the room's far wall and Earle's collection of college pennants and the large map of the world voodooed with redheaded pins through the heart of every city Earle will visit on his sabbatical from Caltech or M.I.T. or someplace like that. He peels his face off the plastic mattress cover—a bumper sticker separating from its backing.

Errrrrrrrr-rle, croons a too sweet voice from outside his door. It's time to wake uhhhhhhhhhh-up.

Oh Kaaaaaaaaaaa-ay.

His penis now makes a small white tent of his underwear, so Earle walks to his room's bathroom slowly, in place more than forward. Through the plant, the plane, and the rocket there she is, the wife in 10A, in the building's other wing, back already from her early-morning aerobics. She begins her cool-down pre-shower stretches; she sports a sport bra and Lycra knickers, a yellow ponytail, a sweatband/chronometer. Earle runs to his bed, pulls a small wooden wedge from under his mattress, runs to his room's door, wedges it closed (Mom! One second, don't try and force it. It must be swollen from the humidity. Yeah, swollen, he would say if he had to). Behind the large leaves, with his free hand, he tries to unscrew the toothpaste top, pinning it on the sink for leverage, finally opens it, but with an inadvertent ooze into his fingers. He licks off the gel, reaches, wets and puts his toothbrush into his mouth, brushes. Since he is now naked, no one can prove who is the Peeping, who the Tom.

Earle is soon spooning Cream of Wheat into his mouth in the kitchenette.

While his mother reminds him his suit for the B'nai B'rith/NAACP dance at the Copa this evening is back from the cleaners, hanging on her closet hook, I'll tell you what she does not look like:

She is neither fat (her breasts don't swell the lace top of the apron she has never owned), nor has she any gold teeth. She cannot sing, nor is she ever called "Mama" (though that is what she calls her own mother). She does not, not work in public relations and her two-handed backhand is not, not envied by her peers.

■ ■

. . . should be here any minute. I told him we'd go to the zoo.

Yes, I do realize you are sixteen years old, smartypants, but there's no law against sixteen-year-olds going to the zoo. You used to love the zoo. Your father and I would leave you for just one hot second and off you'd go to the monkey house, scratching your armpit and jumping up and down. One time you ran off and grabbed this balloon seller's bouquet of zoo balloons and were already a foot or two off the ground before your father could pull you back down, remember?

Oh, that must be Solomon. Be nice to Mr. Levitt even if you decide not to go with us, okay, sweetie?

Darling, you look like a million bucks, you always look like a million bucks, do you know that? In one of my buildings just the other day I was saying to the super, a lazy worthless EssOhhBee but he's been with me for years, I was saying, I know this woman who looks like a million bucks, says Mr. Levitt, rotating the last half of a cigar between thumb and forefinger before chomping on it again in the side of his mouth. Hey, kid, how they hanging?

Answer him, Earle, answer Mr. Levitt.

After the zoo, we'll get a bite to eat at this four-star joint I know in City Island, you wouldn't believe the crab cakes they got up there, as big as basketballs, then who knows? maybe a movie. My treat. What do you say?

Oh, let's just go on without him, Sol. When Earle gets in one of his moods, I swear. He even skipped school yesterday. I just don't know sometimes.

Solomon Levitt lays his briefcase flat on the dining-room table, fingers the wheels of the combination lock, then thumbs outward the triggers that free the latches to spring. Too bad, sport, but here's a little present. Your ma told me you was into that electronics stuff. He hands Earle a shrink-wrapped Heathkit U-Build-

It multi-tester. And here's ten bucks for the batteries or some-thing.

When Earle's mother says, What do you say, Earle says, Thank you, sir.

. . . and did I remind you to rinse your Cream of Wheat bowl, says his mother, now downstairs, calling on the doorman's house phone. You know how it gets glued to the bowl and spoon like sandpaper if you don't do it right away, and the dishwasher only bakes it in. . . . Promise me you'll get out of the house today. It's lovely outside, not too hot yet, or muggy . . .

The instructions for the multi-tester say it will take nineteen hours for people seventeen years old and older to assemble. It is now ten o'clock in the morning and I'm sure Earle's planning to finish the kit long before tonight's nine o'clock dance.

2

The taxi's quick lean to the stop lifts Earle off the seat as he stuffs the folded dollars into the cab's money slot. She's got to come, Earle says to himself, reaching and reaching again for the car-door handle he only eventually finds.

Thumping interrupts Earle's words. A doorman holding a clip-board caps the disco's entrance. A group of pretty, light-skinned young black women and expensively dressed young white men hurl their names at the man at the door. They walk into the dark, into the beat. Earle speaks his name to the clipboard, twice.

There she is, alone.

A hostess approaching in a short, red, starched dress and emo-tionproof makeup sways between him and her. The hostess offers,

then distributes, tiny scrolls from a tray yoked around her neck
by a strap:

THE COPA

It makes their bodies throb.
The Beat, it thumps, the Beat.
Its pulse still makes them bob
Through melodies and sweating feet.

Reds criss and cross the blues,
They skim the crowds, these discs of light,
Finding mixed heads, yet they lose
The stuff beneath that height.

The strobe flash, hard flash.
Explode. Black. Room. In. The. Thump.
A simple thrust is seen a slash.
A sexy grind becomes a hump.

The chains drop from his throat
Like golden, frozen falls.
He undulates, appears to float,
His pants constrict his balls.

Her miniskirt is more a belt,
A narrow, leather thing.
It rubs her bone, will force a welt,
All just for a fling.

—Bill DePopulaire

Inside the club, Earle's pupils expand with the ripples in the
punch, responding to the beat on the punchbowl. A Jewish mother
with a silk flower on her bosom and a heavy smile scoops fluid
into Earle's two glasses and onto his hand. In this light the drink
is black but tastes red. A black woman mans the hors d'oeuvres
table.

There she is again, dancing with some girls. The crazy lights
darken her hair. Another black young man nears Janey Rosebloom
to the beat, groin first. She turns to him to the beat. They dance
at each other.

The bathroom is warm and clean and empty and quiet. Earle turns the handle that turns the bolt into the hole in the stall door, shakes the stall door, wipes the seat with a pillow of tissue, and sits. The stall wall is patterned with jagged Magic Marker ink (see table 2.1), some of it still wet and thick-smelling. Yet even this doesn't help, so Earle exhales noisily, screws shut his eyes, wrenches tufts of hair, grits his teeth, and stamps his feet.

TABLE 2.1
Samples of Bathroom Graffiti

The color of chocolate and also of shit.
Vidi, Vici, Veni
Janey Rosebloom is Hot to Trot and I know it for a
fact, Jack.

The men's room attendant, a wizened soul whose ebony skin is cracked and creased like some ancient Nubian riverbed that long ago suckled a thriving metropolis, nods toward an empty stall and the better-dressed high-school boys scamper to line up in front of it.

Earle now stands at the sink, along with nerd after nerd, pressing forehead zits from the left and from the right.

Did you see Mary/Naomi/Laraine?/ She's so incredibly beautiful, even better than her sister, but I was such a stu-nod saying, Hi, Darryl, this is Ramona—I mean you're Ramona, I'm Darryl! I could've just died right there/Heather pressed her leg into mine for a good minute and a half, she's got to want it/I just said to the pharmacist, They're for Mike, my big brother. You fill them up with water and throw them off the roof, right?

Earle tries to strut from the bathroom. Seeing Deborah adjusting herself so near, Earle stops and turns. Hey foxy baby would you care to dance, he mouths to himself.

T minus ten seconds and counting.

Earle brushes off his lapel lint.

Earle growls, revving up the vocal cords to prevent voice cracking.

T minus five.

Earle swishes a mouthful of air in his mouth to kill the anaerobic halitosis microbes.

Earle swishes his hands over his head to press down any uneven nuts of hair.

Hey, baby, I could not help but notice you are alone here. May I suggest we too start our own party? I've got some wicked weed with me, says Jamil in gold chains and tight pants. Deborah smiles, pulls him away.

Earle lifts a toast point and tilts it toward the dance floor—the only light in the room. He seems to be guessing the pâté's true color by its red, blue, and strobe-light forms. Shawna tells him he is about to eat *pâté de foie gras,* goose liver. They make it by strapping large wooden funnels to geese throats and then force-feeding them until they vomit, then force-feeding them the vomit. Earle asks her to dance. She says she would rather eat goose liver. Earle gags and gags again, grips her shoulder.

The pâté on the toast at first sticks to his nose, then the bread dangles and falls facedown to the floor. Leaving, Shawna rubs the remaining smudges of wet gray from her fingers onto the wall, her legs chopping through the slits up the back and front of her dress, calling, Bouncer. Bouncer.

The nerds see Shawna, see Earle; joyously they shovel their hands into the pile of liver and the nearby tub of California Onion Dip.

3

Well, Earle's story so far has degenerated pretty quickly, now hasn't it? If you ask me it's got "No Sale" written all over it. But girls, women? Now black women *sell*, according to a friend of mine who works in publishing.

4

From St. Rita's School for Girls, the young women flood, then dribble out the imposing and ornate gothic gates.

Their kilts short, their socks tall, their loafers brown, their blouses yellow or white, from way up here they always look like little candies, delicate balls of assorted deliciousness. In one group of four, walking arm in arm in (etc.), the prettiest is dark brown and semisweet—Dorothy and friends in *The Wizard of Oz*. At the corner, from deep inside their jumbo athletic jacket sleeves that tunnel well after their fingertips, packs of cigarettes appear and are passed around. Ponytails are freed and shaken tangled. Dorothy lays her *Barron's Guide to the PSAT* on the sidewalk before her, bending over but knees ever locked. Her friends also bend and stretch, press the sidewalk with their palms; pull up legs extending to pointed feet high above their heads. Obviously they are dancers.

When the limousine arrives, they quickly snap their cigarettes onto West Ninetieth Street. And though it is now out of sight, I see the long car stopping on Ninety-sixth, where Dorothy pecks her affluent friends, steps out, then down the subway stairs, and into a filthy uptown train.

5

Out of the subway stairway she rises, and rises well. Her bottom doesn't swing too much to be vulgar, just enough to provoke. Her skirt (that skirt! I can't imagine what was going through the mind of the nun who designed that plaid ultra-mini as the uniform for all Catholic girls . . . *Now let me see, one more stitch and yes! Lovely! Mother Superior will be so proud of me. Why, it will almost even cover their little derrieres. Now, surely the dear, sweet, precious young things will be certain of going to Heaven. For as Augustine teaches us, "No girl shall find that pie-in-the-sky without exposing a whole lot of thigh."*) is unique this afternoon on Lenox Avenue. Harlem.

Girl, you better get your black ass out that street and in behind my register like you got good sense, says Dorothy's mother, Darcelle. She will be one of those fundamentalist, tough-as-nails black women who, underneath, are pussycats.

Moms, have I ever let you down, says Dorothy.

Behind the yellowed Formica counter, Dorothy crouches a bit, steps into the orange rayon jumper, and rises, an employee.

Darcelle sucks her teeth as she opens the thick Plexiglas cash-register stall and releases a woman under a hairnet. She says to her daughter, locking her inside the booth, And I want to see you studying them books in between customers. I'll have my eye on you, girl.

Thank you, sir, but no, I don't get off work until *very* late, Dorothy explains to a police officer through the circle of bored holes at her mouth level in the booth. My *mother* needs me here and I have to study *every* night. She eyes him as she plucks from him his bill, spikes it on the spindle tip that is so sharp it twinkles when the light hits right.

I didn't think that birthday party would ever leave, Darcelle

11

says to Dorothy. You finish all your homework? 'Cause I don't have to be explaining the consequences if you didn't. Come on out the box and get youself something to eat. We got some ribs still. They turned out good.

Yes, Mama, says Dorothy, folding closed the PSAT study guide on Part IV, Antonyms. Darcelle unlocks the booth door, and the mother and the daughter grab the long, iron, hooked poles leaning on the dining room's far corner and, outside, hook the heavy steel shades' ends, unroll them over the windows noisily. The narrow metal gate over just the restaurant door Dorothy closes only half down. Her mother, then herself, stoop back under the steel. Dorothy, inside, locks the front door behind them, leaves the key in the lock.

Mommy. Do you think I could head back downtown now? Julie's having some kids over and . . .

Darcelle walks to her office off the kitchen, pulls the top file open, dips in her hand. She slowly presses the silver bowl of the thermometer end toward Dorothy's pressed lips.

Mama! Dorothy's head dances around the thermometer. I ain't sick.

You must be sick asking me if you can go off downtown on a Monday school night.

That ain't funny. You aren't funny, Mother. It's just some friends. No boys or anything. Just a little study group for the PSATs. The girls I have dance class with.

Lord knows if boys weren't going to be around, you wouldn't be calling me Mommy, wanting to go on down there so. You bad as Shawniqua, spend all that money to send her off to Yale University just so she can engage herself to some greasy Frenchman. Besides, Mister Jefferson's taking me to studies tonight, so I need you to look after the twins. He says you just tell him your size and width and he'll get you all the Fayvas you want. I can't understand why you don't like him.

I'll have to call Julie then and tell her my mother's too mean to let me go study with her. You don't care if I fail the test or not.

You can tell that little rich girl to kiss my big black behind is what you can tell her.

Mama, you can be so street sometimes. Dorothy drags down the zipper of her jumpsuit, steps out and out of the room, leaving the orange rayon shell slouched over her metal chair in front of the plate of ribs.

Darcelle stretches behind the bag of flour, pulls out the bottle of cooking sherry, then looks to the corner from where Dorothy will reappear, and swigs.

6

From her throat, past her open lips, scratchy, wet sounds grind out Darcelle's mouth—an orthodontist's saliva pump hooked over your lip, sucking. The shrink-wrapped couch falls in around her; the corns on her feet, which flop on the coffee table, lump her knee-high stockings. From her left hand dangles the TV's remote control. The TV itself glows electronic static. Its crackling/the mother's snores: harmelodic.

Hanging her pumps from her fingers, Dorothy walks barefoot through the white wall-to-wall. Her calves ball tense over tiptoes as the black mini rubs a line in her thighs. The notes from her mother's throat descend as she laps at her own loose saliva. Dorothy stops, starts, watches Darcelle's eyelids. Dorothy squeezes the front doorknob before turning it, turning it just till the lock is freed; then she inhales and squeezes around the door.

7

I'm sorry. I don't know what more to write. This story's just as forced. It's embarrassing to stumble so obviously in so public a forum, but I guess sometimes you just have to throw it up the old flagpole and see who salutes. Things were going pretty well for a while, then somewhere along the line I got sidetracked again. I don't know. It's been almost twenty years since I was a teenager, but I thought it would all come back to me. I was also trying to remember my ex-nieces and nephews (my ex-wife's sister's children)—bourgeois, materialistic miscreants to the one, but I must have blocked them forever out of my mind. I swear that whole family is worth at least a thousand-page historical novel. Summers on the Vineyard, liposuction, tennis, analysis, golf, BMWs, and the Bahamas. If I were the black John Jakes I'd be laughing all the way to my made-for-TV-movie deal.

But as you can see, both story lines—Earle's and Dorothy's—have their problems. Obviously enough, folks, I need help. Anybody out there who's inspired, please write in and tell me which story you like better; and what are your favorite (and least favorite) characters, witticisms, grammatical devices, etc. I promise to incorporate your suggestions and keep the ship sailing smoothly from here on in. Just write to:

"Which Ones Do I Kill?"
c/o Dewayne Wellington
572 West 90th Street, Apt. 10E
New York, New York 10024

I'll stop writing until I hear from you good folks. Luckily, I have to take a breather anyway. Bills are stacking up, so I'm going back to Klein, Klein and Feldman to do some more legal proofreading for a while. Most months I can squeak by, albeit by the skin of my teeth, but Rosa Luxemburg's developed this nasty heart condition (too much ash in the Fisherman's Platter with Cheese Bits) and it looks as if they'll have to operate. Yet it's not nearly as degrading as you might think, becoming progressively myopic scrutinizing the briefs of $400K/yr partners almost a decade your junior. Joyce worked in a Trieste bank, Faulkner was the postmaster at Ol' Miss, and Ellison shined shoes.

Dear Freak,   September 20, 1984

What genus of disturbed, DT-ridden Muse rattles through the chambers of your vacant head? What oh what can evoke such a perverse perversion of pen and ink? Is it that you were encouraged to lick squids as a child? Told it was all right to play with yourself at the school assembly?

Yet enough. For me to further ponder your twisted and undoubtedly sordid beginning causes a sea of revulsion to well within me more thick and putrid than that evoked by any car-smashed rodent or Port-a-John.

"Which ones do I kill?" you so needlessly and smugly ask. My answer shall be as brief and as precise as the turbulent storm of my incensed thoughts will allow.

Yet I will not answer with the word you probably expect—"Yourself." Nay, instead I say all the women in your grotesque menagerie should be "killed"—liberated from your sweaty and pitiful grasp.

No, we women of color do not need your atavistic brand of representation, thank you.

                                                Isshee Ayam

P.S. Here is how you should have commenced your "work."

CHAPTER ONE REJOICE!

Earle awakened to a day as new and as fresh as Mama's hand-starched and sun-dried petticoat, a huge, plain garment as large and as fresh-smelling as the revival tents that bloomed every summer along Route 49 in Lowndes County, Georgia. Yes, from out of those wide Baptist thighs, thighs that shook with the centuries of injustice and degradation, thighs that twitched with the hope of generations yet unplanted, thighs that quivered with the friction of jubilant, bed-thumping, and funky-smelling lovemaking, emerged Earle.

Yes, Earle pulled his lanky-but-still-growing arms and legs out of that big old bed, from out of which—just sixteen years before—his mama had screamed and squeezed him to life. The old gray-and-white-striped but fresh-washed and feather-filled pillows of Mama, Maylene, Nadine, and Lurlene still bore the hills and valleys of well-needed use, though the makers of those hills and valleys had long since been lifted, triumphantly, to begin yet another grueling day of womenchores, back-breaking and unrewarding save for that inner, God-inspired knowledge that someday "The Gates o' Heben will fin'ly open up fo' me."

Yes, Earle stumbled off to that weathered but jubilant and noble handmade cedar outhouse, and as he smeared his adolescent buttock on the weathered gray-and-white-freckled iron seat with 1928 WORLD'S FAIR: PROGRESS FOR PEACE emblazoned on both its face and its underbelly, Earle rolled his eyeballs down Route 49, as he did every morning, vainly searching for the gin-reeking silhouette of his father, who had thumbed his way out of Lowndes County that drizzly autumn morning two years before when Mama triumphantly proclaimed to the family, waving Earle's just nocturnally weighted and fecund-smelling underpants high above her head and the heads of her jubilant, strong-willed daughters, "He is a man! Good God, he is loaded!"

"Way-all," drawled his father coolly as he slung his other pair of coveralls over a shoulder once bitten by a Natchez floozy, "two men in dis fambly be one man too many." And with that, that disgrace slouched North to the land of gambling, drinking, and "fine, light women."

Yes, Earle reapproached the home and peered through the glorious and defiant screen door, mashing his boyish face against the cool plaid of steel. And though he could see, the overly boyish boy did not understand why the women were weeping over a too small but triumphantly hard-earned pile of coins worn shiny; why the big, clean beds that once stood so proudly in the gloriously noble household had vanished; why their stove had been replaced by a tin can and a pipe, though the four deep and worn grooves where their ancient and majestic Franklin had once gloriously squatted still attested to its former fiery presence. He did not understand why dark and thick curls of clouds were rapidly racing toward them.

And yes, Lurlene was perhaps the first to see the cardboard-colored and wrinkled forehead of I. Corinthians just before he smashed back down on his sweaty head his grimy straw fedora. She jerked Earle through the good and hand-hewn doorway while Nadine second-naturedly reached for the well-oiled and well-worn shotgun, whose butt rested comfortably on her shoulder like the base of the fiddle she would never again play since her father had swapped it for "a good time" in Baldwin.

No, I. Corinthians did not continue relentlessly pistoning his shushing legs into the dusty earth to squeeze some other share-cropping family of rent they did not have. Instead, he and his "high-yeller" self turned up into that noble homestead's front yard, crushing the proud spring grasses, babies, under his too

17

expensive Dallas Dogholders and kicking each of the three dogs, Abe, Moses, and Jesus, in those parts he so envied as they instinctively and courageously nipped at his skinny socks.

"It's that time, ma'am," said that shame.

"God Almighty is gazing down from his triumphal firmament, and would you like to know what he is uttering concerning you?" boomed Mama. She drew breath through her sweet but now flaring nostrils noisily, her enormous and kind bosom swelling like the Sea of Galilee.

"Ma'am, its Time," said he flatly, his eyes snaking around the valiant property coldly, cruelly assessing the few articles left.

"You realize completely, Mr. Corinthians, that since the time my husband abandoned us I have had to take piecework and sell all my personal belongings to your employer regardless of sentimental or nostalgic value," she boomed again, her voice as deep and as rich as the Mississippi silt into which, she firmly believed, God had once breathed.

"I tell you this not for your pity," she continued forcefully. "For I know you possess none. I am merely suggesting that, as the Book will inform, 'and ye shall ne'er squeeze blood from any rock.' "

I. Corinthians once again removed his putrid hat, revealing once again that paper-bag forehead, then smeared a snot-laden handkerchief, produced from out of his seersucker breast pocket, across the dried-up wrinkles of spite—riverbeds long lacking the rain of human kindness.

"I am a generous man, but y'all knows that when Mr. Wyte wants his money," he slurred, "he wants his money."

"We-have-no-money," the fierce lioness proclaimed flatly, while that I. Corinthians merely sucked his yellowed and rotting teeth.

For long, hard moments they stared, two burning mare's eyes against the two bloodshot pink eyes of an opossum.

The 'possum's eyes strayed to the mare's bosom, then down to those still fertile thighs enlivening the plain calico print.

"Maybe ah c'd smooth things ova wid Mr. Wyte," he said, sucking his teeth once more, making the rat-squealing sound that fitted him so well.

As Mama blinked the beginnings of tears back into her eyes, her voice now strangely hoarse, she whispered, "Children, leave me and this—man—for a short while." Maylene and Lurlene and Nadine ran to their mama's side.

"Out!" boomed the Nubian Queen.

High above, the wrath of the Almighty churned the heavens into a turbulent whirl of shapes, sound, and power as the triplet pillars of sisterhood wept tears of acid that burned their noble and once joyous cheeks into horrific masks of despair. The long and stout dirt road was first freckled, then drowned by the deluge of the firmament's frenzied furor, the wind's howl shuddered the splayed kudzu leaves and shimmered the tall Georgia pines' many slender fingers high above the weeping daughters, as if trying to shelter them from the mysterious monsoon. Earle simply threw rocks at a proud wizened oak in the rain, while Jesus, Abe, and Moses hid 'neath the stately porch, their shamed paws covering their weeping and downturned eyes.

I'm speechless, Ms. Ayam. How can I thank you for dragging my meager tale back to its roots in Afro-American glory-stories? As a token of my profound and heartfelt appreciation, please accept this juicy, choice list of a few of Earle's favorite things:*

*Sung to the tune of John Coltrane's "My Favorite Things," Atlantic SD2-313.

All kinds of tanks, Janey Rosebloom, Cream of Wheat, neighbors,
Corinthians, toast-r-waffles, his own bean-fart vapors,
A tightly-tucked-in bed,
Chef Boy-Ar-Dee,
Schefflera, balsa wood, and Pay TeeVee.
Eff. Ay. *Oh*. Schwarz, linger*ie* straps, cowboy boots and hats.
Snuggle sacks, Chap Stick tubes, BeeBee guns, and films!
Sci-fi, cars, dance—Slurpees.

Jamaican accents, cleavage, efficiency, artificial cheese-food prod-
uct, romance, haircuts, ankles, livers, the way a pretty woman's
high heel dangles insecurely from the big toe of the crossed leg
always nearly falling or—from a slight kick—flying spike-over-
toe—an exotic Oriental weapon; but never doing either, just dan-
gling, the toe of the shoe covering just enough to promise, Fer-
raris, Lamborghinis, movies with guns, adventure novels at least
slightly grounded in a base of historical fact, watches that cal-
culate, chirp, and play games, computerization, being sick enough
to lie in bed all day, but not sick enough for his mother to tuck
a trash bag under his chin like a green lobster bib, and three
wastepaper baskets, one on each edge of the bed, bread, warmth,
ant colonies and farms, sweaters, bikinis, calendars, Lauren perfume that he thinks smells like sunshine, ties, kindness, solder,
flame, the two dimples resting over each of a woman's buttocks
straddling the spine, Christmas, World War Two, pretending to
jog, Riverside Park, not this restaurant, not Lenox Avenue, but
a double helping of chicken livers and gravy and grits and rolls,
thank you.

9

Well, what you gonna have, sweetcake, or you just gonna eat with your eyes.

Are you still serving brunch?

Chile, for you, ànything. She squeezes his arm. But you gotta hurry up, I got a full boat in here now.

A double helping of chicken livers and gravy and grits and rolls, thank you.

BISCUITS AND VISCERA, WET AND FAT.

Darcelle moves to the other tables, wiping wet circles as she passes. The menu (table 9.1) is long and plastic-coated. Many notes are attached to the top edge by paper clips.

TABLE 9.1
Transcription of Chez Darcelle's Menu

	ENTREE	VEGET.	DESS.	PRICE ($)
MONDAY	Vienna Sausages au Jus!	Corn, Waxed Beans, Spinach	Jell-O	3.75
	Tender pinkies of choice pork parts smothered in their own anti-botulistic gelatin			
TUESDAY	Platanos Fritos!	Corn, Waxed Beans, Spinach	Jell-O	2.99
	A special taste treat for and from our Latin brothers. Imported plantains deep-fried in our specially selected peanut oil			
WEDNESDAY	"Fillet of Soul"!	"	"	5.25
	One of the best-known and best-loved members of Afro-American cuisine—chit'lins, or chitterlings, as they were once called, carefully			

	cleaned and selected for taste and texture			
THURSDAY	The Jupiter!	"	"	4.65
	A delicious ball of ham food ringed by a fresh slice of canned pineapple			
FRIDAY	The Gibraltar!	"	"	1.75
	Two whopping pounds of cornmeal mush fried in bacon drippings. A hearty king-sized treat			
SATURDAY	*Boeuf* Darcelle!	"	"	2.10
	One of our favorites. Only the choicest FDA colors and flavorings go into this veritable culinary smorgasbord			
SUNDAY	All of the Above!	"	"	2.00
	To celebrate God's day, we'll offer you any of the above delicacies—at a heavenly price!			

10

What does Earle make of this curious ensemble of foods?

God, what a weird place. Mom'll kill me if she finds out I ate up here but hey bud you only live once, you know what I mean [laughs]. Geez, you laugh like a fucking goon, that's why that guy's staring at you he's thinking, Why is that sweaty fat kid laughing, I bet he's crazy, he's thinking. That's what the lady in the cash-register booth is thinking too, I know it but God, Earle, why the fuck do you worry about what an old lady with plastic-perfect hair says. Oh shit, plastic-

perfect hair! That's a hairnet you stu-nod, what if you'd gone up to her and said, My, madam, your hair sure is orderly, she'd've laughed or killed you or something, geez crapola is what it is, God how'd I get way up here anyway, I bet I'm miles and miles from home, oh what is it? Miles to go before I weep? . . . no, shit what a friggin' airhead you are, no wonder you only got a eighty nine geez. Oh crap were your lips moving again, God I'm sure nethead is looking now she's probably pressed some friggin' button under the counter to call the cops that's why she's pretending to be so bored, shitfuck, she doesn't care anyway I bet that booth can take a four fifty seven no sweat BLAM *but a red dog heat-seeker anti-tank weapon would pop it open like a cherry, heh heh. Don't touch that button lady, I'm telling you hands up, nope? Okay zzzzzzzzzzzzzzzzzffffffffffppppppppp right for the red on your cigarette and* BOOOOOOMMMMCHHhhhtcxtc *not even enough pieces to put on this wacky menu. Heh heh. Boy if people knew the real me, psycho killer teen . . . Hey! Wait! He's my only son officer and no I don't know where he got that assault rifle or how he got to the top of Riverside Church (though we've been members for years), when suddenly* BLAM*, down goes the old lady upstairs who hangs on my arm to get in the building without even asking like we were going out or something, yeah probably some babe saw me and was thinking, Yeah I'd like to sit on his face and marry him but he's going out with that scrotum-skinned douche-bag grandma. Scrotum-skinned, I'll have to remember that one 'cause that's just what the old lady looks like only no hairs. Where's my food? I don't want to be killed up here . . . Shit Earle, lighten up will you? You're not a fuckin maniac, you're just, well, emotionally disturbed, heh heh, yeah, just think about it, three, maybe four steps to being committed, just stand up—nobody's looking—hop on the table—now they're looking—whip out your little wienerschnitzel then drop a load right on the chicken livers if they ever get here, I could do it I know it ready one two three. Stop fooling around and just look mean so they won't know you're not from uptown. Yeah, iss cool whussup yeah. Shit Earle they spotted*

you a half hour ago. Yeah there he is the black Howdy Doody face,
I bet he's got lots of bread on hisself—bread? Do they still say that?
Now wait, here comes the waitress so act normal, ready here she comes
T minus five four three two

Uh no, thank you. I don't drink coffee, thank you. *I don't*
want any of your shitwater or brown dyed menstrual juices, what if
I'd said that it would've been great, me and my Howdy Doody face
just smiling and saying that and at first she'd not get it because she'd
think she had me pegged then the bottom of her face would just drop
and she'd say Did you say something? and I'd say What and she'd
scratch her head and as she waddled away I'd whisper Shitwater and
she'd straighten up and turn but I'd be eating like nothing's wrong, then
turn to look at her like What seems to be the problem officer and she'd
go in the back and drink a bottle of booze which she was just trying
to quit. Now what. Let's bob the old head to some funky beat, that'll
make them think I'm cool. Yeah I'm rappin inside me that's how cool
I be, shake your groove thang shake your groove thang yeah yeah yeah
baby come on and shake my grooved thang, that's what I'll say to the
lady when she comes back. Anything else sweetness? Yes, as a matter
of fact, I'd like you to shake my grooved thang please, with your
tongue if it wouldn't be any inconvenience. EARLE *what the fuck is*
the matter with you, that's why no one will ever go out with you you
freak not because you're fat but because you're Krazy oh this must be

Thank you.

Hmmm ain't bad some soul food up in Soultown then I'll watch
SOOOOOOOOOULTRAAAAAAAIN brought to you by the Johnson Com-
pany, makers of Ultrasheen, Afrosheen, and Ultrasheen cosmetics and
here's your host DDAAAAHN *Cornelius clapclapclap. Eat, but first look*
around, nobody watching, good, act like everything's A-OhKay and
spear the turd and swirl it in the diarrhea then scoop up some maggots
and eat two three four delicious and repeat and the rolls? Rat brains?
Pterodactyl turds? No, larvae cakes, a delicacy they are considered
in some cultures, three four

Water? Yes please.

What now? Oh how can I forget Love Afro-American Style, and now our first contestant is a Mr. Earle Tyner who hails from New York City New York State. Yeah, it's a pleasure to be here Bart. And it's a pleasure to have you here, well shall we get started Earle, all you have to do is look out this window here and spot ten ladies you could have sex with if they asked you or grabbed your crotch or something and you win! Ready—begin. Uhhhhhhhhh the one in the Lycra pants isn't bad bodywise but her face is ugly. Nope I'm sorry lady I have to say no but wait maybe in the corn rows but yuck too fat. Hmmmmm slim pickins here. Oh I guess I'd take the one with her hair up and light skin. MMOOOZZ Well I'm sorry Earle you didn't name all ten, in fact you scored lower than any previous contestant but we won't let you go home empty-handed, oh no. Johnny tell Earle here what he's won. Sure thing Bart. Earle, you didn't get the grand prize but you will receive a lifetime supply of world-famous Oreo cookies! By Nabisco. Nabisco: where we bake for your sake. Don't kid yourself loser you'll never get anybody black or white. Why don't you just get it over with and marry your friggin' right hand.

Oh no, they were good, very good. I'm just thinking, that's all . . . No, madam, don't bother. I like them cold (swallow/gulp) mmm-mmm.

Anything else dear? Some more rolls? Jell-O? . . .

So, honey, where you go to school? I can see you at one of those fine West Side private schools like my girl. She at Saint Rita's, but I can see you all in a tie and jacket, though I just met you just now, but I can tell you gifted . . .

You is the slowest eater I ever see, but that's all right, because we ain't that busy now atall, and besides, it's good for you to chew things thoroughly instead of just throwing them down your throat like most folks do, not even tasting nothing, like a steam shovel . . .

You don't mind if I sit here for a minute, do you, baby? The other girls can hold the fort for a while, and my feet swell up so if I don't rest them . . .

You not from up here, I knew that straight off, so you be careful, and when you leave go straight down Lenox to one twenty-fifth and don't pay no mind to what nobody say, because they just want your money and nothing else . . .

Sure you don't want no Jell-O? I got blue . . .

I already said you bright, and don't think I'm trying to take advantage of you or nothing, but my toaster's not working, seems only half the bread gets done at a time and it takes too long to turn it around and get the other side done. . . .

You got a girlfriend? You know, a girl. If you don't mind me asking, love, 'cause well, one of my girls is a Yale graduate but the other, she goes to Saint Rita's, like I said (don't have no Phillips head, but sometimes a small regular screwdriver'll work if you careful. Make sure it's unplugged now). Anyway, she a little wild now, what with that group she frequents, but deep down under she's real sweet, and I was just thinking you should come back up here after school someday and I'd introduce . . .

I knew you could do it, why thank you, and here, take this pie and don't even dare think of saying no. Shoot, it's not home-made anyway, but it's Entemann's which is almost . . .

Don't you forget now what I said about you coming over after school, baby, and be careful out there. So long, sugar.

12

The next day, Earle finds himself in school. At homeroom he and the rest of Mr. Morgan's 10E wait for the end of Mr. Wyte, the headmaster's, morning announcements before bumping to get the good seats in their first period classes.

In Junior Varsity lacrosse, Friends 0, Carver 10. Better luck next time, men.

Earle sits in the front of homeroom ahead of Janey and next to his friends Donald and Andy. They call themselves "Base 3" or "Trinary," but others just call them "Nerd One, Two, and Three," the numerical assignment predicated solely by the order of appearance. My generation in the sixties might have dubbed them "Rainbow Three" because their skin tones fan from Earle's brown to Donald's beige to Andy's white.

Base 3 now wiggle to the side of their chairs closest to the door, their right hands twitching, just a bit, over their day packs' grab loops as the second hand of the quartz-commanded wall clock robots into nine.

*mmm*MMMOOZZ

Already closest to the door, Andy is swinging around the doorjamb, slinging himself into the corridor and scaring some girls. Earle is just behind and Donald soon after. In trying to brake and corner, all three slide wide, scare some more girls, then push each other into the computer room.

13

Donald says he's got dibs on the Wang, but Andy says, Homo you don't, and just sits at the terminal, turns it on just to bug Donald, because Andy really likes the DEC VeeDeeTee better. Earle sits next to Andy on the right, like he always does, and Janey walks in, her books over her chest, and sits right in front of Andy, like *she* always does. Earle told them how he pretends to have six-million-dollar bionic zoom eyes, so each blink increases the magnification on her sundress, until he is inside the yellow pattern and in heaven. But now Commander Considine, Commander See they call him, looks at his watch and closes his door just on the bell, so he can stare at the late people as they try to come in quietly, but the bumpy glass window on the door is loose, so no matter what, it rattles loud like it's about to smash.

Janey's already confused—she's more the artsy type—and raises her hand like a Nazi and says, Commander Considine, Commander Considine, but he just keeps on saying junk about making sure that the FOR isn't too big or else the NEXT loop might become infinite, which is obvious, and now Janey's arm is tired and hooked over her head like her hairband and she's waving at the Commander from over her other ear and breathing real loud on purpose, and every time she waves, her chest stretches her sundress, and Earle wouldn't be surprised if her boobs one day just pop right through the fabric like sinus medicine capsules pop through that foil backing.

Earle sends a message over to Andy's terminal, because all three of them have rigged them up so they can write to each other *and* Commander See, while the other kids can only send to the Commander so they won't cheat, so if Trinary get caught they'll be in a shitload of trouble, but sometimes you just have to go for it, right? Earle's message is this:

because Andy and Donald were on the Island so couldn't tell him this weekend, but Andy just types back

HEY, DON'T SWEAT IT, BUD.

Then the Commander's finished explaining something, and of course he looks right at Earle and says, Mister Tyner, we missed you on Friday, and Earle's of course real embarrassed, but Considine can be a real asshole sometimes, so he asks Earle to send his assignment to the Commander's terminal, and naturally Earle's like crapping in his pants when Commander See looks at his monitor and goes, Thank you, ah, a text editor! A very ambitious undertaking indeed. Earle's all weirded out, because he didn't send anything, but Andy and Donald look away and hold their mouths, then old Considine says he assumes Earle also provided a text for them to edit, and asks Earle to send it to him right away and he'll send it back out to the rest of the class's VeeDeeTees and again Earle looks all panicky, but Commander See's looking at something scrolling up his screen (you can tell by his bouncing eyes) and says, Ah, science fiction.

THE SCREAMING WARLORD RENEGADES
OF THE BORAN NEBULA
by Earle Tyner

[So you even wrote it yourself, says the Commander, and Earle looks at Donald, who's shaking his head real fast.]

"Battle stations! Battle stations!" cried the yeoman as the dictatorial starcruiser bombarded the tiny renegade starfighter. The trusty starfighter crew scrambled all over the place to their laser cannons and were giving the behemouth starcrusier a real run for its money.

"We've been hit! We've been hit!" cried a crewman as sparks went everywhere and the whole ship rocked a lot, but the brave renegades blasted and blasted for all they were worth. But it was too late. The behemouth starcruiser had already activated its ion-propelled tractor beam so the tiny spaceship could not possibly escape even if it gave everything it got, which it did.

"Men," said the mighty warrior renegade commando chieftain Stonechin McQuaid, "lay down your weapons. We'll have to use our brains and our wits to get out of this onx. Leave it to me and I'll show that girl, that fiend Princess Wickedheart Janxp, that we will never give in to her and her likes!!!!!!"

[The kids laugh, especially Janey, who says, This is great, and smiles at Earle, so Earle smiles big at Andy and Donald for making him look good, but Donald's eyes are all open like he's being mugged again and he's saying, Control See with his mouth slowly and big but without noise, but there's no way Earle's going to stop the run now and try a different text, what with Janey's starting to get hot and want him. Andy's just smiling at his screen.]

"Here we go right into the belly of this evil thing," cried the ship's first science officer. "Boom!" the renegade commando starfighter banged into the huge ship's inner dock. They could hear a lot of running around outside, then KABOOM! the front hatch blew up and vaporized, and outside there were thousands of dictatorial guards with their blasters pointed right at them. Janxp rode up in a chain-and-snakeskin bikini on her Ussex, a huge, armor-coated lizard, all flexed and oiled.

Considine says he thinks that's enough, and says let them run the edit program now to see how it works. Earle looks straight ahead at Commander See while Janey's looking at him, and his chin is tilted up so she won't notice the sack of fat that usually hangs there.

Considine's typing, and the whole class receives

YOU HAVE JUST PATCHED INTO TEXT EDITOR 101P SPELLWRITER / PARASHIFTER, WHICH FUNCTION WOULD YOU LIKE TO DO FIRST?

Commander See picks ParaShifter and rearranges the paragraphs.

"Here we go right into the belly of this evil thing," cried the ship's first science officer. "Boom!" the renegade commando starfighter banged into the huge ship's inner dock. They could hear a lot of running around outside, then KABOOM! the front hatch blew up and vaporized, and outside there were thousands of dictatorial guards with their blasters pointed right at them. Janxp rode up in a chain-and-snakeskin bikini on her Ussex, a huge, armor-coated lizard, all flexed and oiled.

"Battle stations! Battle stations!" cried the yeoman as the dictatorial starcruiser bombarded the tiny renegade starfighter. The trusty starfighter crew scrambled all over the place to their laser cannons and were giving the behemouth starcruiser a real run for its money.

"We've been hit! We've been hit!" cried a crewman as sparks went everywhere and the whole ship rocked a lot, but the brave renegades blasted and blasted for all they were worth. But it was too late. The behemouth starcruiser had already activated its ion-propelled tractor beam so the tiny spaceship could not possibly escape even if it gave everything it got, which it did.

"Men," said the mighty warrior renegade commando chieftain Stonechin McQuaid, "lay down your weapons. We'll have to use our brains and our wits to get out of this onx. Leave it to me and I'll show that girl, that fiend Princess Wickedheart Janxp, that we will never give in to her and her likes!!!!!!"

Commander See's smiling and seems real happy and says he's going to try the SpellWriter now. Andy raises his hand and Donald does too, both of them stretching out of their seats like they are trying to fly or something. But the Commander just goes, Not now. Not now, boys.

SPELLWRITER WILL CORRECT ALL YOUR SPELLING MISTAKES BY UNDER-LINING THE WORDS IT THINKS ARE WRONG AND SUGGESTING A FEW NEW WORDS. THE COMPUTER'S GUESS WILL BE BOLD AND FLASHING. TO ENTER THE CORRECT WORD, SIMPLY RETYPE IT AND THE COMPUTER WILL AUTOMATICALLY CORRECT ALL FUTURE REFERENCES TO THAT WORD.

"Battle stations! Battle stations!" cried the yeoman as the dictatorial *starcruiser* (stargazer, stark naked, BAR CRUISER-bar cruiser-BARCRUISER)
STARCRUISER

bombarded the tiny renegade *starfighter* (starfish, star-
STARFIGHTER

[Considine says this fanciful text is a bit difficult to edit, but it would be impossible to program the computer to differentiate between real and imaginary words.]
their laser cannons were giving the *behemouth* (Plymouth, Bassmouth, BEHEMOTH-BEHEMOTH-BEHEMOTH)
BEHEMOTH

[All the kids in class go *Awww* and the Commander says, Excellent. Good work. How many of *you* students knew how to spell it?]

starcruiser a real run for its money.
[Commander See says, Notice how it's not requerying already corrected words. Magnificent, Earle.]

"Men," said the mighty warrior renegade commando chieftain *Stonechin* (Stonewall, Ston-

STONECHIN

McQuaid (McDon-

MCQUAID

, "lay down your weapons. We'll have to use our brains and our wits to get out of this *onx* (onyx, ONE-one-ONE)

ONE

I'll show that girl, that fiend Princess *Wickedheart* (Wick-

WICKEDHEART

Janxp (jinx, JANEY-janey-JANEY)

[Now the Commander's about to type Janxp, but the whole class is shouting JANEY! JANEY! JANEY!]

JANEY

[And everybody cheers and Janey just shakes her head and blushes real beautifully, and Earle stretches out his chin even more.]

then KABOOM! the front hatch blew up and vaporized, and outside there were thousands of dictatorial guards with the blasters pointed right at them. Janey rode up in a chain-and-snakeskin bikini [lots of laughing]

on her *Ussex* (usher, Essex, PUSSY-PUSSY-PUSSY)

[God, like the entire class is screaming and screaming, then Considine goes and types

PUSSY???

but the computer doesn't read the question marks.]

a huge, armor-coated lizard, all flexed and oiled.

Janey whips around at Earle and is all red, but it's an angry red, not embarrassed, and Earle's almost gray and must think her eyes are laser blasters or something, 'cause he jumps and ducks at the same time, but like a goof lifts up his desk and his VeeDeeTee slides off it in slow motion, like all big expensive things do before they break, and Earle tries to catch it, but he slips and twists out of the way just before it could smash his leg and KUSHHHHHHCHHH-

33

ppop the whole thing crashes on the floor and the tube implodes and glass bits go flying everywhere tinkling, and Janey screams, My leg! My leg! There's glass in my leg, and she jumps up but doesn't knock over her computer; only her skinny shoulder strap on her sundress catches on something and rips her top and her right bra right off, and there it is, and Earle's already halfway out the door with Andy and Donald pushing him even faster, but now Earle stops dead, even though her hand is over it, holding it now, but he is like petrified and won't budge, though his friends are really leaning into him, and Janey pulls her top back up, and Trinary falls all over itself and out the door, in a running pile.

14

I can't fucking believe it, I just can't fucking believe it. Andy tells me to lighten up it was just a joke they weren't absolutely sure how it was going to correct which is a lie. Shitcuntpissfuckfuckerpigshit my life was already shitty and they had to go on and ruin it some more. No, Commander Considine this is not my idea of a joke, I just did not want to get my friends in trouble is all and besides I wouldn't've done that to myself and to her not for a million bucks. Gee I wish I'd said that to him instead of just sitting there in Mr. Wyte's office just choking and wheezing on my own tears like a wimp. Shitfuck don't curse so much that's why noboby likes you, nobody likes you because you're fat and crazy and a Peeping Tom pervert that's why, oh please let the whole class be vaporized by a thermonuke before they can spread the word so I'll never have to ever see them again. Jesus Christ I'll be forty years old and some venture capitalist or something when some kid'll come up to me asking for drug blackmail money or else he'll spill the beans and I'd be on skid row cleaning car windows with a snotrag instead of paying up, but I'll just change schools that's what I'll do, go to Pee.Ess. One sixty three and get stabbed and boofed by gangs in the bathroom and die and there'll be a little note in the FriendsShip class notes saying Ex-student split in half in public school. The End. Oh Jesus Christ I walked right past my street like a goon like I've not just lived there only all my life, Mom, shit she's going to go apeshit when she finds out, they probably already called and she's got Dr. Sheldon all ready to shrink my head and everything, he's probably there for dinner to get us all reacquainted, now isn't this nice.

15

Earle, you're home. Now, before you say a word, Mister Wyte called and explained everything, and I've got a good mind to call Misses Williams and tell her what a little monster her Andrew is, Firestone Science Fair winner or no Firestone Science Fair winner. Of course, he and Donald will pay for the computer, because what they did to you nobody else would have done to a dog, let alone best friends. But come on in now and change, I'm taking you out to dinner, you choose the place. That's the least I can do after what they did to you, those retard-looking science monsters . . .

Are you sure you want it rare, honey, don't you think you want it just a little more cooked—worms, you never know—and besides, that's how I prepare it at . . .

Oh, here it is, and doesn't your steak look wonderful. I wish I had ordered that, but isn't that how it always is. Besides, you know what red meat does to my pancreas . . .

Slow down, baby, you eat all hunched over your food like your grandfather, and we've got nowhere to . . .

Look at that woman over there, behind you, the fat one. Why, look at her arms, like bags of mashed potatoes. If I ever get like that, Earle, why, you just shoot me and sell the meat . . . Why, thank you, Handsome Harry. You know you're quite the charmer when you want . . .

Look at him, next to the hostess. I bet he's a model or something, he's just too good-looking. What do you think? . . . I know you're not a homo, but that doesn't mean you can't appreciate the beauty in someone, and don't say homo, say homosexual, and don't say that either . . .

Did I tell you about my day yet? Work was miserable. Seems some bomb was found in the Johannesburg airport, didn't go off, thank goodness. Well, anyway, the press came around as usual asking us if we thought it was safe to travel on EssAyAy and what was I supposed to say? No, don't fly with us or you'll be blown to smithereens, and then where would I be? Where would you be? Not here eating rare steak, that's for sure. And seriously, it's less dangerous than flying to Miami or even Houston, or anywhere else that's just a stone's throw from Havana or *Habana,* as they say. Of course, if they thought it was really dangerous, they would have told me and I would have told the pressdogs, that's what we call them, *pressdogs,* because that's just what they're like, especially with us. But you know what they call us? Oh, I'm sure I've told you before, *flaks,* you know, you've got all that World War Two stuff, public relations is like the flak vests pilots used to wear to protect them from—what do you call it?—shrapnel; that's it, shrapnel. Must be German, shrapnel, sounds like schnapps or schnauzer—Oh, how ironic! A bomb almost goes off and me, I'm a flak!! . . .

Oh my God. No, this time don't turn around yet. It's Erica from *All My Children* sitting with—oh, you know—who's the one who played the cripple in *Coming Home* and the male prostitute in that cowboy movie. Oh, you're too young to have seen that—Jon Voight! That's it. I wonder what they're doing together. Nope, still don't turn, they're looking right here! Oh Kay, now. Aren't we two terrible [laughs]. She's looked better, but I guess on the show they have people that all they do is decide what they wear for them; still she's kept her figure together, which is more than I can say for him, will you look at those chins! . . .

You know, if your father were here you know what he'd say, don't you? Nothing in here but no-good rich white folks with nothing better to do then spend ten dollars on a two-dollar piece of meat. You know I'm right, but we had some good times, didn't we? Nassau. You remember our first time to the Bahamas, don't you? Of course you do, but then again you were only just a little baby boy. Or Omaha Avenue in Columbus, and what's her name, LaCreta the babysitter that drank. I'll never forget your father opening the door to find her bent over that old ugly print couch, the one we gave to your Uncle Miles for his summer house upstate, her naked behind all up in the air and that boy right there, and glasses of your father's fifteen-dollar-a-bottle Dewar's in both their hands! [Chuckles] Oh, you're too young for me to be telling you this but [chuckles] I'm sure if she hadn't drunk up all his booze he wouldn't have fired her. But he did like his liquor, we both know that. You're old enough to talk about this, aren't you? You had to live through it, and that's enough to age anyone, and you've handled it very well, yes, you . . .

Oh, my goodness! I've been meaning to ask you how the party was. I remember as a girl we used to have the best parties, food and punch, but nobody would dare spike it because those mothers were something else, let me tell you. And if some boy was dancing too close to his girl? Why, those mothers would just stop the music, just snatch the needle up off the phonograph, march out there, and throw the boy out on his ear, oh yes, they would! But

I guess they're not like that anymore. I bet some of those chaperones were teaching you children a thing or two. *Children*, listen to me, of course you're all very fine young adults, ladies and gentlemen, but I can't help it. To me you're still babies, and don't you ever forget what Grandmom always told me, "No matter how big you get, you'll never be bigger than me." . . .

Are you sure you don't want dessert, honey? You know you love their french-fried ice cream, and we can split it, because summer's just a month away and I refuse to be seen on the Vineyard with these thunder thighs, and you probably don't need the extra . . .

Sure that's it, sweetie? Tea? All right then, when our waiter—Bart, isn't it—comes around, do me a favor and ask for the check . . . Because it'll be good practice for you, that's why, you're the man of this family, don't forget. What'll you ever do on a date? Have your girl do all the talking? Besides, it's . . .

The maître d's sort of a snob, don't you think? You know, that good-looking Arab . . .

Let's make a real evening of it and take a taxi home, but I just hope he's not Korean. The last time I got into a Korean cab I said "Riverside Drive," then I looked around me and we were halfway to the River Club way over in Brooklyn Heights. He took me home for free, but still . . .

I know it's not the right time or place, honey, but how are you feeling? You know [whispers] Doctor Sheldon's office called just last week. I didn't want to tell you then, well, you know. He says he's got Fridays at four free and that's right after school, and he's right there on Seventy-eighth . . .

Oh, honey, don't bother checking the mail, I picked it up this afternoon, nothing for you today, I'm afraid. But don't worry, I'm sure that Wellington fellow hasn't forgotten. He'll write you soon. He's a man of his . . .

Earle honey, I know you get embarrassed talking about it, but how do you really feel about me going on dates, I mean really? We can't have any secrets between us two, we're all we've got . . . Are you sure? You know it's not that I go out often, and I never bring them here even when you're away, but it's just that I'd like to remarry someday, not too soon, God knows, but someday. I miss your father and I know you do too, but sometimes, and this may sound awful, I think he's better this way. He was sick, Earle, he wasn't happy, not one minute of the day, not one minute . . .

Good night, Handsome Harry, and don't stay up too late, we don't want you missing any more school. Oh, and Mister Wyte and Professor Considine assured me they'd deal with those two. Something about losing privileges next year . . .

And one more thing, Earle. Remember to close your shades. The doormen tell me there's a Peeping Tom in the building.

October 28, 1984

Dear No-Rate Hack:

I must have been naive to have believed that after comparing my work with your own puerile, misogynistic, disjointed, and amateurish ejaculations (and I use the last word deliberately), you would have never again dared to defile the temple of black literature. The only consolation one can derive from your pathetic pornography is that it is so terribly bad that even the seamiest to vanity presses would retch at the thought of ever publishing it.

Of my next installment all I can say is, "Read it and weep."

Isshee Ayam

CHAPTER TWO

SUNDAY GO TO MEETIN'

The next morning's sun woke the heavens with a friendly warmth and glow that told all the earth's creatures that Sunday had finally and so gloriously arrived. Mama leaned over the makeshift stove, frying a spoonful of cornmeal mush and reboiling last week's coffee for her and her grown daughters. But for Earle, their seed carrier, their hope, Mama squeezed the last drops of milk from the shriveled and near-spent teats of their wizened goat, Sojourner.

"Come on now, children, there's a time to sleep, a time to eat, and a time to give to God," Mama thundered.

Six strong, big, and clean feet marched across the wood floor worn smooth by generations of sharecropper births, deaths, pray meetings, and shindigs. Maylene, Lurlene, and Nadine stood before the mirror, hanging over the washbowl—as if such a tiny piece of reflective glass could contain three such jubilant images! But no, they did not need a shard of silvered glass— Mama's meager wedding present from Uncle Ike in Chicago— to tell them their looks. Instead, each combed the others' hair, washed the others' cheeks with the practiced ease of good sisterhood.

"Come now, boy," said Mama as she shook Earle's lazy shoulders. "Don't make me have to whip your behind this holy day and make your butt drip blood and pus on my good clean sheets from now until the day Gabriel blows his mighty horn!" said Mama with that all-kind, maternal fierceness that knits black families together tighter than white on Carolina rice.

Out of bed and into the brisk Georgia morning, Earle turns away from the women and they from him as he nestles his young manhood into the crotch of his wool Sunday britches and slides his father's still-too-big gambling shirt over his corpulent but still growing body.

The family, like all the others around Lowndes County, all wearing proud, old clothes, pressed and starched and bleached respectable, walked down Route 49 toward the swelling hums and organ clouds of Sunday spirituals that surged from the clean white doors of Mt. Zion Baptist Church. Inside, the barefoot congregation swayed and fanned itself in the rising spring heat as the lean and ancient preacher crept to the pulpit, two deaconesses at his side and the smell of corn liquor on his breath.

"Friends," began the preacher. "I can call you all friends, can I not?" Some responded, "Yea," others "Preach on," and still others the time-honored "Amen." "These times are hard times, mighty hard times, times so hard we think we're not going to make it; times so hard we wonder does anybody out there care; times so hard we think nothing good's going to come our way. I say times harder than our soil after that drought of twenty-nine, times more lean than a two-dollar Porterhouse steak but tougher than ten-cent chuck, times even more stressful and contrary than that Great War that took so many of our proudest sons, times of trial and tribulation. I said trial and tribulation. But are these times for giving up?"

Most chanted "No" or "Uh-uh," but Mama rose to her feet to utter in a voice deeper and richer than any man's: "Not as long as there is blood in my veins and breath in my bosom."

Cheers, applause, foot stamping, and hollering burst from the congregation as if I. Corinthians and Mr. Wyte themselves had just passed away on the Fourth of July.

"Thank you, Sister Pride, thank you," said Preacher as the commotion subsided. "I believe we can all learn something from this monetarily meager woman who is spiritually a billionaire! No, I don't believe our Sister Pride would trade her faith and her lovely young women and her fine young man for *all* of Jonathan D. Rockefeller's riches. And neither, and neither, I say, would any of you if you are truly possessed by the word of our Lord God Jesus Christ. Can I have a witness?"

More deep affirmations raised from the rapt congregation, as Miss Pitman at the worn organ began "O Lord My Rock, My Only Word."

After the service and after the deaconesses had thoroughly revived those special souls so taken by the spirit that they collapsed in the aisle, this jubilant community rose to its feet to sing once more—not so much to a distant God—but more to sing to themselves, to their own strength of will to overcome no matter how oppressive and unjust their world; to persevere no matter how many I. Corinthians and Mr. Wytes crossed their well-traveled paths; to—in the words of that old Afro-American spiritual— "Keep on keepin' on."

"And before you all go, my children," continued the preacher, "to gather with your families and praise his name, let us all welcome two newcomers into our humble, joyous flock. Mrs. Darcelle Lamont and her daughter Dorothy, formerly of Macon County, but the good Lord has seen fit to now bless us with the presence of two such upstanding and God-fearing disciples of our Lord God Almighty Jesus Christ, amen."

The new family stood proudly next to the preacher at the church's tall and strong front doors as the congregation poured out its warmth and hospitality through their firm, noble handshakes or heartfelt hugs and in return smiles as big and as happy as melon slices beamed from the two women's joy-filled faces. Yes, "women," for Dorothy possessed a keen intellect and understanding of this world far beyond her sixteen years. So as she shook the hands and hugged back those who hugged her, she saw the real tears in their eyes. Tears of joy and of true spirit. So as she breathed in the intoxicating perfume that only stately Georgia pines can bestow upon this world, and as she looked out onto the Georgia hills rolling to the sweet horizon, her thoughts wafted to heaven itself; tasted the sweet communion wine still purpling her tongue; felt the cool gingham blouse gently rub her just-sprouting buds; buds that would soon swell into breasts; breasts that would lead her away, one day, to Atlanta, the lost city submerged by centuries of injustice whose own sin once ignited and consumed that city in the fire and wrath of the souls it had so thoughtlessly destroyed; destroyed but not dead, for it was those very souls that rose again from the flame to found a new city and a new university; yes u-ni-ver-si-ty! Oh, how that sweet word smelled and bloomed, exploded in her head! That school on a hill through whose gates the great women of color would pass, and one day soon Dorothy herself would pass and become the first black female J.D.-M.D.-Ph.D. in the history of our land.

CHAPTER THREE
GOIN' FISH'N

Earle and his two friends, "Cornbread" and "Bassmouth," snuck out the back of that wise old church just as the congregation rose to greet the two new women. There, behind the shoulders of that bright, clean house of God, the three boys hid behind the tall, proud oak—God's oak, the simple, kind folk of Lowndes County called it. Then they scampered silently, crouched low, their poles nearly touching the ground, almost as if they knew that just six years later all three would be crouched low, silently scampering over a landscape not their own—only this time the fishing poles would be rifles and the land would be Alsace, and instead of a friendly competition between the boys, the winner receiving a cherry Coke, now they'd all be fighting in the second war to end all wars and no man would be the winner—

Far enough from the church, they whooped and hollered, patted their hands on their mouths like Native Americans, chased the squirrels and chipmunks into the trees, and sent the quail and pheasants scurrying and bleating through the woods. At Sinner's Creek, Bassmouth pulled off his white, stiff-starched church shirt and untied the rope holding up his pants to expose a light-brown band of flesh spotlighting his exaggerated sex. Then he swung on old man Fogarty's old tire swing into the translucent blue springtime creek water.

"That Bassmouth sure is a crazy feller," said Cornbread.

Earle and his friend pierced, then slid the thick, squirming nightcrawlers onto the rusty hooks—poor and lovely slaves conscripted into the adolescent baiting of proud, beautiful, and innocent fish. The two boys then both lay back on the cool Georgia moss, their straw hats tilted lazily over their faces, long stalks of sweet grass gesticulating slowly from their hidden mouths with every lazy chew.

Just then Bassmouth came running back, winded.

"He's coming, he's coming! Les all head fer de hills!" he screamed.

"What you young pick'ninnies think you doin'," screeched old man Fogarty. "Fishin' and runnin' 'round buck nekked out cheer on my prop'ty."

As he spoke the wizened black ancient's face creased and wrinkled and crinkled with every injustice that had ever slapped the glorious elder warrior. His shotgun, near as old as himself, rested comfortably in his arms.

"Get outta here, you lazy, good-for-nothin' baby nigguhs," screamed the old man, his last word revealing how deeply his twisted wound of a lifetime of racist oppression afflicted him.

And they ran, oh, how they ran! The wind at their backs urging them forever forward and away, away from the misdirected self-hate of previous glorious generations. Now deep in that so-sweet-smelling woods, they collapsed, out of breath, laughing.

"Shoot, Bassmouth," said Cornbread. "If LaQuita know'd how outta shape you is, she'd drop you like a hot potater."

"Don' you go holdin' yo' breath now," replied Bassmouth, " 'cause I know you done got the sweet-eye on her."

"That stringy old mule?" he replied. "Why, I wouldn't touch your skinny yaller gal with a ten-foot fishin' pole."

"You wish you had one!" replied the other two in practiced simultaneity.

After the laughter died down to a quiet murmur of soft guffaws and huffs, Cornbread asked seriously, "But, Bassmouth, whut's it really like?"

Earle held his breath.

"Whut's whut like, l'le boy?" laughed Bassmouth.

"Y-y-you know darn wail what he's talkin' 'bout," stammered Earle.

Bassmouth then sucked his teeth, hooked his thumbs in his beltloops, took a deep breath, and threw out his chest. "Oh-h," he began expansively, "it's hard to get at, but once you get it, it mighty fun."

"What do you mean, 'hard to get at'?" asked Earle tentatively.

"Whut I mean is dat if dey don't wants to give it up, ya just gots to take it. But dey likes it better dat way anyways. Besides, yuh kin usu'ly tricks 'em into doin' any thang you wants." Bassmouth belched.

"Like what?" asked Cornbread, surprised.

"Well, let's say she says she don't want to 'cause she knows you's just gonna skididdle on her and the baby and she'll be all 'lone with dat youngin' in Lowndes while you's ovah in Memphis or some such place with dem tree-dollah hoores or up Norf all rich and fat, and she be on relief all her life 'til she die. Wail, if she ups and says all dat gibbledypie, you just tells her a big old bumblebee done stung your weeniewanker and kilt all yo' sap!'' Bassmouth laughed and laughed, his face twisted into a hideous death mask of ugly stupidity as the other two hesitantly chuckled, just vaguely understanding through the near-impenetrable cloud of youthful, hormonal ignorance that something just might be amiss.

The muted gong of an age-old, time-worn skillet being beaten by a much-used, wizened old spoon could be heard skittering through every corner of that fresh-smelling forest, like the spirit of God herself. And soon behind that sound the deep, fiery boom of a voice all too familiar to Earle calling out his name as loudly and as proudly as the day she squeezed him from her loins.

So yet again he ran, but this time not from a wrinkled face ancient yet hardened by time and injustice, but to a force, a well of strength more powerful than any shotgun blast, lynchers' dogs or firehose puke. And there she was, as he would always remember her, looking out over their barren yet triumphal paltry acres, her thick, kind hand saluting the horizon as she scanned the woods for her only son, one thin wisp of sweet-smelling smoke streaming out of the tall, noble chimney forever skyward, a telegraph to heaven, his mother always said, and behind her his glorious sisters, unrelenting breakwaters between him and the vagaries of a society he had never invited to come and agitate his gloriously simpleminded though priapic cosmos.

FOUR

SCHOOL DAZE

Earle pushed off the patchwork quilt, still warm from the other bodies that had since left it, and prepared himself for school.

He poured himself a cupful of water from the chipped but immaculate enameled pitcher into the stout washbasin and lathered his hands with the cake of homemade soap as he asked, "Y'all already eaten?"

Mama looked sternly at each of her strong daughters, then said to Earle, "Yes, now eat yours before it becomes cold."

The half-filled tin plate steamed with the palm-sized dollop of navy beans and the tiny sliver of salt pork. In two spoonfuls the food was gone, and a moment later Earle's matchbox-sized square of cornbread had sopped up the film of lard on the plate's smooth tin bottom.

"More please, Mama," he asked. "I'm starved."

His mother swallowed hard, then buried her face in her apron while Nadine ran to comfort her, Maylene snatched away his plate, and Lurlene washed it noisily.

Outside, the red Georgia clay on Route 49 coolly reassured Earle's still-growing bare feet as he silently marched the fifteen miles to school. Every few minutes, silhouetted in the red-dawn glow of the horizon, a small cloud of dust would race toward him and slowly grow into a truck. In the cab, two white men, their shotguns on the dashboard, and in back, iron slat sides and a chicken-wire dome transporting fivescore of black manhood to yet another place to dig a ditch, build a road or bridge, or trim Mr. Wyte's hedges or mow Mr. Wyte's lawn.

Eight miles down the road Earle heard the slapping of running feet behind him.

"Howdy, Earle," huffed Cornbread. "I weren't even goin' come to school atall 'til my ma sicced the switch on me."

By this time the sun was fully awake, the beads of dew had already ascended from the curtains of kudzu vines hanging from the stately oaks, and that ever-fierce and ornery Georgia turkey buzzard circled lazily in the vault of heaven. Earle and Cornbread walked on.

"Earle?" Cornbread broke the silence, " 'member what dat Bassmouth say to us yest'day?"

"Whole lot of nonsense is all I remember," replied Earle.

"Wail, I-I been thinkin'," continued the morally weaker of the two excitedly. "Actually, I been doin' lot mo' dan jes thinkin'."

Earle looked at Cornbread for an explanation, but kept marching forward—toward learning.

"You know how my cousin Lucinda and her mama's been living with us ever since her pappy done run off wid dat jazz singer from Mobile. And you knows how I been feeling awl funny 'bout the way she be wearing no clothes whan she bed, even though she close ta ten years old? . . . Wail," he said, "we done it."

Earle stopped quickly; a puff of red dust rose from his startled feet.

"With your little first cousin?" asked Earle incredulously.

"We done went behind de outhouse and I done told her to close her eyes cuz I gots a surprise—"

Earle started walking again, his legs now pistoning quickly into Route 49, desperately, so desperately trying to distance himself from the sexist ignorance that lay behind him in such over-abundance; not just in Cornbread or Bassmouth, but in so very many of the inhabitants of that glorious, triumphal, venerable, jubilant, and God-fearing yet backward place. But despite his revulsion, torrid confusion rocked his thoughts, as if a divining rod lay within him and he was not yet sure which way it would gesticulate.

The schoolhouse bell was ringing and Earle could see the forty-eight-star flag skitter up the tall white pole as the little children filed into the little room first, then the ten-year-olds on up to the oldest students, all marching inside that humble hive, that haven of scholarly advancement; all the students pledging allegiance to the flag, but not really to that flag, more to a future flag, not only with more stars but with new, invisible stripes, colored rainbow stripes earned by the blood, sweat, and tears of all those Selma grandmothers firehosed into history.

"Well, class," began Miss Johnson's hope-filled voice. "The older children will begin their assignment on the middle of page 24 in *The Narrative of the Adventures of W. W. Ellis as a Former Captive in North America.* I hope you all remembered to bring your copies . . ."

Just then Cornbread and Bassmouth noisily burst into the tiny schoolhouse, eyeing Earle suspiciously.

"You are late again, gentlemen," reprimanded the teacher. "Take your seats, and, Charles, you begin."

Bassmouth sat sheepishly as he slowly unfolded the thick paper.

"M-m-m-my f-f-fir-r-r fir-first d-d-d-d-day, *day* of fr-e-e-dom, *free*dom," he began, pausing, pained, wincing. "Wuz th-the day I l-l-l-learned to read."

The tiny triumphal classroom nearly burst with laughter as Bassmouth crushed the paper, looked down at the table, and viciously kicked his desk. His face radiated shame.

"I am very disappointed in you boys," pronounced Miss Johnson.

Cornbread unfolded his copy noisily, thrust out his chest, and raised his hand high in the air in that temple of advancement.

"I'll show you, Miss Johnson," he said snidely.

"Very well then, Paul," she said. "Proceed."

"My first day of freedom was the day I learnt to read," recited Cornbread as he quickly refolded the paper and beamed triumphantly.

"Very good, Paul," she said, feigning surprise. "Continue."

Cornbread gulped and looked up at his frowning teacher, his eyes wide with shame and with ignorance. He whispered, "I kin't."

"Louder please, we cannot hear you, Paul."

"I kin't," he repeated between sobs.

"Earle, your friends seem to need your help," she said. "Do you think you can read it?"

"I don't know," he replied sheepishly. "But I'll surely try." He straightened himself in his seat and carefully opened his pages of that encoded treasure.

"My first day of freedom," he began, his voice shaking only a little, "was the, the day I learned to read . . . I-it w-was not, as you m-might suspect, the day I ar-arrived in New York a free man, nor was it the day I spoke to our President, Mr. Abraham Lincoln . . ."

"Excellent, Earle," said Miss Johnson gloriously. "Unlike your friends here, you have improved quite steadily. Excellent."

Earle's cheeks, like Bassmouth's and Cornbread's, burned, but his embarrassment was of a different sort.

"Anyone else like to try?" the teacher asked.

In the front, a delicate hand rose steadily roofward, not waving impatiently, but firm.

"Very well, Dorothy, continue where Earle left off. Children, I believe you all met Dorothy and her mother at church yesterday."

With a reassuring nod from the teacher, Dorothy began: ". . . Abraham Lincoln. No, it was the day the school primer that I was forced to hide under my straw bed ceased being mere scribbles and scribes and miraculously metamorphosed into sense and meaning and truly wonderful tales. I shall forever be indebted to Mrs. Jonathan V. Cumberlake of Nantucket Island, Duke's County, Massachusetts . . ." And on and on Dorothy read in a voice small yet sure, her back to the others up there at the front of the class, she nevertheless filled that magical house of learning with a power, a vitality, a spirit, and a hope it had seldom seen before. Young and old students listened raptly to the wonderful words that flowed surely out of the new woman's mouth like an endless stream of golden treasures.

Miss Johnson beamed. "Where on earth did you learn to read so well?"

Dorothy replied gently, simply, "My mother taught me."

After geography, recess, and arithmetic, Miss Johnson dismissed the school but asked the two who filled her with hope, Dorothy and Earle, to stay after. As the other students ran out the door laughing and playing, and as the young and handsome teacher went back to her office to get the two special books for the youths, and as Earle approached the front of the class—just then, Dorothy stood up and she, too, moved into the aisle.

"Oh!" they both harmonized. "Excuse me," they said again in concert. Then each smiled at their mutual folly and each proclaimed, "You go first," at the same time. Again they laughed.

"You read real good, well . . . Dorothy," said Earle to the floor.

"So do you . . . Earle," said Dorothy, also into the clean hardwood floor.

By the time Miss Johnson arrived with her gifts, the two young seekers each felt a strange yet wonderful surge well within their souls, yet exactly what that unshakable, mystical force was, both Dorothy and Earle were not yet at all sure.

■ ■

Mr. Wellington, I trust even you can handle the narrative from here.

Dear Ms. Ayam,

I sure can, and I can't thank you enough for more of your oh-so-generous assistance. What else can I give you in return except an even longer and less readable list.

—D.W.

16

It's the Friday after Earle's embarrassing Monday. He hasn't been to school all week. Instead, he's watched shows like *The $25,000 Pyramid,* where celebrity guests give contestants examples and the contestants must name the category described:

Casino Royale, The Newlywed Game, The Dating Game: films and game shows sporting themes both written and performed by Herb Alpert and the Tijuana Brass. *Bing!* [applause]. Beds, legs, sweaters, clocks, draft beer, tables, slot machines, all science-fiction robots, roads, caves, most formal organizations, potatoes, lettuce, corn: inanimate objects referred to anthropomorphically in everyday speech. *Bing!* [applause]. The trigger, the barrel, the sight, the butt, the infrared nightscope: parts of a high-powered, anti-terrorist rifle. *Bing!* [applause]. Tortilla Flats, The Mud and Soot, The Grime and the Weasel, The Grits and Sweat, High Tex-Mex, Pork Parts, Celery Stalk Slims, The Weight Watcher's House of Soul, the House of Meat and Meat By-products, The

House of Stabilizers to Preserve Freshness, Picaresque, Arabesque, Montesquieu's, Perfidy's, Eat, Wang Ho's Palace of Macrobiotic Tortes, any restaurant whose last name is "Too," Chicken Feed's, The Domestic House of Grilled Meats, Just Another Restaurant, Yet Another Restaurant, One More Restaurant, Too Many Restaurants, What? Another Restaurant, My Brother's Other Restaurant, Not a Bad Place to Eat, An OK Eatery, The Other Eatery, The Eatery Next Door, Down the Street—An Eatery, Two Blocks More, On Your Left After the Light—So-So Dining, The New York Eating Company: A Tradition Since 1984, You Gotta Start Sometime: A Tradition Since 1983, The Steak Factory, The Fish Factory, The Manhattan Food and Drink Works, Inc., J. J. Pinbody's Feed and Grains Co., The Fashion Plate, The Silver Plate, the Golden Plate, One Potato, Two Potato, Beggar Man, Thief, Three Blind Mice, and One Heckuva Cook, Chic? Chez It Isn't So, ... Go On to the Next One. (*Awwww.*) Prince Andrew, philosophers, prostitutes, wife-beaters, dogs that continually hump their master's leg or the legs of complete strangers, people who always hold the door open for others, news anchorpeople who always appear earnest and caring, presidents of corporations and nations, some houseplants (studies have shown), fish that don't burst away when you tap on the glass, Bassmouth, homing pigeons, ornithologists, actors, anyone who says God bless you/*Gesundheit* after a perfect stranger sneezes, nurses, some doctors, den mothers, most blood donors, hypochondriacs, all Peace Corps volunteers, nerds, anyone who smells their just-washed-and-dried clothing, smiles beatifically, then clutches them to their bosom, anyone who bakes, mail carriers who whistle, all police officers, firemen, and emergency medical technicians, tons of beauticians, Miss Johnson, honest used-car salesmen, singers, Peter Pan, career shoes salespeople, naturalists and their ilk, florists, masseuses/eurs, artists, models, the beauty queens who ride atop pastel-colored convertible Cadillacs and believe a sincere wave is a quarter rotation of a cupped hand, game-show gift presenters, demonstrators, delivery people who really, as soon as their customers open the door, push their army officer–style hats back on their heads, smile more broadly than natural, and say *Mornin'!*, traveling salesmen/women, small children who accept candy from strangers, people who travel long and often, Peeping Toms, Donald and Andy, anyone who forces their squeamish friends to accompany them to horror movies, everybody who *loves* Gilbert and Sullivan, or has memorized every postwar show tune, girls who swoon, Northerners who wear Tony Lama lizard-and-armadillo-skin boots, animal trainers, daredevils, Darcelle, your food server for this evening, a lot of fine clothiers, child pornographers, psycholog(chiatr)ists, fathers who in real life slowly withdraw their pipes from their mouths and ask their sons, *So how was basketball practice today, sport?*, my childhood friend and his theory of systematically squeezing one's intestines upward to release a fart out the throat, Americans who spell *colour*, white rastas, black preps, rastas and preps, the guy at a laundromat who would offer someone else money for that old shirt, then rip the shirt in half and wash each half in leading detergents *to prove a point*, and how about those who unconsciously say "y'all" when speaking to directory assistance in the South, assimilators, phonies, perverts, malcontents, Earle, all customs inspectors everywhere: Why, people looking for love, of course. *Bing!* (applause). Dog food, uh, Cuisinarts, ap—*mooozz.* I'm afraid your time is up, and though you don't win the whole kit and kaboodle, you won't go home empty-handed . . .

17

It's ruined, it used to be so great but now it's wrecked . . . Hi Earle, this is Janey Rosebloom. Can I pretty please with sugar on top be tutored by you in programming? Yes [pant] I'll come over around eight because your mother is away somewhere for a very long time and we'll have her king-sized bed and shower massager all to our lonesomes for a week or even longer. Oh my it's warm in here you don't mind if I disrobe while you teach me about bytes, like this one I'm giving to your earlobes (har har) right this very moment in the shower while you massage me all over and we grab each other's heads and kiss, and now fill me with your lance of love that's so totally humongous I'm gasping with disbelief . . . MY LEG, MY LEG! THERE'S GLASS IN MY LEG! I'D NEVER TOUCH ANYONE WHO DISFIGURED ME!

18

This time Earle talks to Andy and Donald on the phone, three at a time, because Donald's dad's a doctor so has this three-way calling thing. They've been calling all the week that Earle skipped school, but he just never answered. Now it's the weekend and he's cooled off and they talk about tomorrow's PSAT and Donald and Andy say they'll spring for Earle's Pay One Price ticket at Coney Island and even a knish or corn on the cob or something, because it's the least they can do, seeing he wasn't now never going to bang old Jancy Rosebloom or nothing.

This is their first time at Coney Island this spring, but last year they used to go almost every weekend and play Skee Ball until they won some of those pens you turn upside down and ladies' ink bikinis slide off, but once Donald won a set of booze glasses you're supposed to put ice in, and in about five minutes the glass sweats and their whole frosty bathing suits turn sort of invisible, only they'd just pour water on the bikinis to speed it up, and finally they just scratched off the frosting altogether, only that put lines in the ladies' tits.

Andy and Donald tell Earle about this wicked Ferrari Three-Oh-Eight GeeTeeEss they saw burn up Third Avenue and nearly go right under a truck. Earle tells them about the Lotus Esprit he saw parked on Riverside Drive with a license plate that said PTOU, and Stavros in Beginning Calc says that's Greek for fuck, but Andy says that's impossible, they've got people whose job it is to know all the dirty words in every single language to stop people from doing just that. But Stavros is a Greek fucker, so he should know.

They buy their tickets from this fat guy in the booth who keeps on laughing through his nose like a snake's laugh, *ssss ssss ssss.* Next they go get food, because Coney Island food is all really good and you can't find it anywhere in Manhattan at all. Andy buys Earle a knish like he promised, and all three get hot dogs at Nathan's, because it's world-famous and has been at Coney Island since back in the olden days when Coney Island was clean.

Pull his finger, says Donald, grinning a lot, and Earle says, No, his farts smell disgusting, like he's sick or something, and they stopped doing that stuff when they were kids, and even if they were in the middle of a friggin' tornado his farts would still smell rancid. Donald pulls his own finger and cuts an EssBeeDee* anyway, and Earle and Andy walk away like they don't know him and Andy says back at Donald real loud, you farted, and this old lady next to Donald turns at him like he's a mutant, and he runs and catches up with Earle and Andy and calls them both faggots,

*S(ilent) B(ut) D(eadly)

and Earle looks at Andy and sniffs and says there is a humongous fungus among us.

The three of them are still hungry, so they get a super-jumbo order of french fries, the ones that come in the foot-tall paper cup with the french-fry pictures all over the outside. Andy eats the last one and Donald and Earle bitch. Andy says tough shit and Earle says chew harder.

There's no line at the Cyclone, because most people are wussies and would have heart attacks or something right at the clackety-clackety-clack, ratchet-like noise when you're being pulled to the top of the big hill so slowly that all you can do is think about the roller coaster that flew off the tracks last summer and killed a bunch of Explorer scouts in the South somewhere, but the scariest part of all is right at the tip-top, when you're sure you're going to fall out of your seat and land on the tracks at the bottom just in time to get run over by your friends screaming with their hands up in the air to prove they're too cool to hold on to the safety bar. But after the bottom of the first hill when your jaw is relaxed again, it's just a cool ride, because you know if you lived through the big one you can live through the hills and curves until the end.

Let's go again, says Donald, but he doesn't need to, because they always go twice even though it's not nearly so scary the second time.

After the Cyclone they do the go-Karts and Earle beats Donald for once, because for some reason Donald is like a freaking Mario Andretti in a go-Kart, while Andy just gets mad and tries to drive them into the old half-buried car tire safety bumpers lining the sides. Then they do the Haunted House and some other kiddie junk just to get their money's worth out of the PeeOhPee tickets.

19

Trinary's on the train back to the city to see a movie in town, but it doesn't start for another forty minutes, so they head to Swensen's for milkshakes. They've got to get Andy psyched up to pretend he's seventeen, since the movie's an *R*. It's not nearly so hard anymore, seeing as they have only one more year to go, but back when they were fourteen and fifteen it was real hard, they'd have to speak real deep and talk about cigarettes and sometimes even had to pay some old bum a dollar apiece to pretend he was their legal guardian.

The ice-cream girl is a fox, Puerto Rican, with long black hair and dark eyes. She looks like Jennifer Beals, that actress, only short. Andy says he's going to go over and ask her when she gets off work, and Donald and Earle say bullshit at the same time, and Earle says pinch, poke, he owes him a Coke, and pinches and pokes Donald, but nobody's ever paid out the Coke ever, and anyway, Andy's been saying stuff like how he was going to pick up all these girls since a real long time and he's never done anything at all except once with a real dog at Camp Winamac who probably did it with horses she was so skanky. Then Andy says that sure she was not half as good as all their babes, right? Like their five point eight times ten to the fiftieth *Playboy* centerfolds they've had that all look like their fists or socks or tomatoes, or whatever else they beat their meat with. And Donald asks how would he know so many ways to meat-beat if he weren't the world's record holder himself. Andy says he guesses he will be going to the movies alone, because he is the only one without a little baby face that can pass for seventeen, and he will tell them all about it tomorrow after the PeeEssAyTees.

Andy takes off his glasses and unbuttons his shirt to his belly button and half closes his eyes, like he is high on drugs. Youse gots any cigs in dare? he asks the ticket lady, even though Earle told him it was stupid to talk like he was from Brooklyn, and of course she says no, so he asks for *tree* tickets and a couple of beers, and Earle swears the lady looked at Andy like he was a real jerk.

The theater is like a French palace, with curtains over the movie screen like it was a real theater. Everybody inside is their age and most of them are guys. There are even a few goons from Friends who see Earle and yell Falconjaw Quarle! and crack up, almost having conniption fits they're laughing so hard. Earle, Donald, and Andy give them the finger right there in the middle of the theater. The lights, then a bit later the talking, go down.

AUTHORITARIAN BUT PLEASANT (V.O.)*
"Welcome to the exciting, wonderful world of motion-picture entertainment. Talking while the film is in progress is disturbing to those around you, so please be quiet . . . Now sit back, relax, and enjoy the show."
Black. "The following PREVIEW has been approved for ALL audiences."

PERKY MALE (V.O.)*
She is the fiery first female President of the United States . . .
Cut to:
Full-screen snapshot of a pretty but serious WOMAN.

PERKY MALE (V.O.)
He is the arrogant and handsome young Soviet Premier . . .
Cut to:
Full-screen snapshot of a swarthy but serious MAN.

PERKY MALE (V.O.)
What happens when these two hardheads lock horns in their first summit meeting? . . . They fall in love. "*Foreign Affairs.* A very diplomatic romance."

Black. "The following PREVIEW has been approved for ALL audiences."
Fade in:
EXT. HIGH SCHOOL—DAY

*V(oice) O(ver). An off-camera speaker or narrator.

DEEP-VOICED MALE (V.O.)
Welcome to Zachary P. Smith High School summer session. It's a very ordinary, run-of-the-mill institution of higher learning . . .

Cut to:
Four YOUNG GIRLS *in gorilla suits leap into the math classroom and hit the* TEACHER *with cream pies in the face.*

DEEP-VOICED MALE (V.O.)
Where the teachers really care about their students . . .

Cut to:
OLD LADY TEACHER *punches* FOOTBALL PLAYER *in the testicles.*

DEEP-VOICED MALE (V.O).
Where the students really care about learning . . .

Cut to:
Three GUYS *sit around a detonator ready to blow up the school.*

DEEP-VOICED MALE (V.O.)
And where everybody cares about having fun . . .

Cut to:
NUDE GIRL *taking shower behind a bumpy glass shower stall. Her nakedness is obvious but obfuscated.* FRENZIED FOOTBALLER *in uniform dives against the door.*

DEEP-VOICED MALE (V.O.)
SUMMER SESSION. Featuring music by the Cars, AC/DC, Van Halen, Cyndi Lauper, R.E.O. Speedwagon, Rick Springfield, Spandau Ballet, Duran Duran, Mötley Crüe, Eddie & the Tide, The Del Fuegos.

Black. "The following PREVIEW has been approved for ALL audiences."
[I love it when they show lots of previews, says Andy, like always.]

GRAVELLY MALE VOICE (V.O.)
The streets are a mess, pimps and pushers rule the city . . .
Fade in:
Side view of a .357 Magnum held by a strong male hand. It begins to rotate.

GRAVELLY MALE VOICE (V.O.)
Something's got to be done *now* and there's only one man who can do it . . .
The gun's barrel is slowly turning toward the Point of View.

GRAVELLY MALE VOICE (V.O.)
Dirty Harry is back and dirtier than ever . . .
Now the barrel is open-mouthed toward the POV.

GRAVELLY MALE VOICE (V.O.)

HAND CANNON
Black, just before a loud gunshot BOOMS, *then reverberates.*

AUTHORITARIAN BUT PLEASANT (V.O.)
"Lowe's Theaters are proud to present our FEATURE PRESENTATION."
[Earle bets it'll be good, that girl from *Doin' It* is in it. Then the
screen's black again, but you can hear the crackling of the movie
about to start.]

Fade in:
Titles on black:
COMPUTER CAMP—where the system's not the only thing going
down.

Donald can't believe they can put that right on the screen and
wonders why some religious group doesn't protest, but Andy
explains that the people who made it would just say, We don't
know what *going down* means to you, but we're talking about
computers, and if you think it's dirty for some reason, that's your
problem. Earle says talking while the film is in progress is disturbing to those around you, so please shut your traps.

The movie begins with this girl in a cabin at night who hears
a noise outside and goes to see what it is, and then she gets super-
scared for some reason and starts booking through the woods all
terrified. She slows down after running a long way and looks
behind her and sighs in relief, then she turns back to see this
huge guy whose face is all in a shadow, then they close up on his
hedge clippers and go black. Then they say, "Ten years later,"
and do the credits over all these station wagons dropping their
kids off at Camp Software. Most of them are real nerds, guys that
look almost like retards, but there are a few normal guys who
look like Trinary will look in a month at *their* computer camp
after school is out, and of course there are some great-looking
girls in cutoffs and plaid shirts, with the shirttails tied over their
belly buttons like hillbillies. They run to their cabin and their
tits bounce all over the place, then in their bathroom they take

showers and change their clothes while the guys peep through a hole they drilled in the cabin's side a minute before. One of the girls has the greatest body Earle has ever seen in his entire life, like a statue, only delicious, and she's taking a shower forever and soaping herself all over and Earle scrunches down into his seat and stares and stares at her, because Miss September Ola Ayim, who used to have the most perfect body ever, he's just discovering has too-skinny arms and real ugly feet and it's like looking at his grandma almost, he's so used to her, but *this one's* going to be fantasy fuel for a week. Donald whispers that her tits are lopsided, and Earle and Andy say that it is just because he's a homo, but then even Andy says she is a little chunky but he would not kick her out for eating crackers in bed, but still, that blonde next to her he would pork until the cows came.

20

Home? You want to go home *now*, Earle, it's only seven-thirty. Why the hell do you want to go home? We could even go to another movie if you want. Or—I got it—let's go over to Donald's house and watch his brother's porno in slow motion on the VeeSeeAre . . .

C'mon, Earle, it's all new stuff, my brother just got a fresh batch of tapes last week and keeps hiding them in a plastic bag inside his toilet. How obvious can you get. And besides, my folks are out in Sag Harbor until tomorrow night . . .

Nobody but wimps study for the PeeEssAyTee, and besides, they're just practice anyway, and you're not even supposed to study, you're not even supposed to think about it, then just jump in and take it so they can tell how smart you are without doing nothing . . .

You know what, Andy, he's going home, but it's not to study, that's for sure. He's going home to whack off to Miss Thunder Thighs in the movie, before he forgets what she looks like. You better slow down, buddy, or one day you'll jerk the skin right off like the sleeve on one of those pocket umbrellas, and there you'll be with this bloody dong trying to tell your mom you fell on an electric pencil sharpener.

21

Gray desks and chairs on gray rubber mats stripe the glossy, hardwood basketball-court floor. The glass bricks in the walls burn white and the ten lamps hanging from the high, high ceiling—all as big as tin trash cans—hum under the talk of the nervous sophomores.

Please take your seats, people, says Mr. Morgan as he taps the chalkboard rolled in especially for the occasion. This is the Preliminary Scholastic Aptitude Test or PeeEssAyTee, as you prefer. If you are here for any other reason, I bid you good day. [The students all laugh simultaneously, producing not one big laugh but a low, warbled hum that rattles the windows.] Today I am not Mister Morgan your Thespian Arts instructor or Mister Morgan your homeroom babysitter, I am Mister Morgan the Law. I am the head proctor of you twenty-score miscreants, and I intend to fulfill my duties utterly . . . By the way, if you do not know what *miscreant* means, I shan't assist you. For your sake, I hope the word does not appear in the vocabulary section of this examination. [More window rattling.] You shall have three hours to complete the examination. After one and a half hours there will be one break of ten minutes. Other than during that break there will be absolutely no talking, palavering, or chitchatting whatsoever. Your answer sheets are being distributed forthwith. You shall not, I repeat, not, touch them with your finely sharpened number-two pencils or any other marking instrument until you are explicitly told to do so. Once these sheets are filled out, you will each receive a sealed test booklet. If your test book's seal is broken, you will have exactly thirty seconds in which to inform the nearest proctor. Failure to inform him or her of the tampered booklet in time will result in your being asked to leave the test premises. [The combined whispers of fear do not rattle the windows.]

As I mentioned earlier, and as you all undoubtedly know, a number-two pencil and only a number-two pencil may be used to complete this examination. Any marks made by other writing instruments will not be read by the Educational Testing Service computer and you will receive no score. Do not mark the answer sheet other than in the loci provided, otherwise the computer may misjudge your answers and thus lower your score. Of course it may also raise your score, so the less bright of you may just be providential. You may mark the test book if you wish and use it for scrap paper; however, since it is not graded, any answers not transferred to the answer sheet are answers unseen—hence, useless. You may look at your neighbors' answer sheet to your plagiaristic heart's content, but it will not assist you in the slightest, since there are many different versions of the tests, hence no one in your environs will have an answer sheet that even remotely resembles your own. Some of the questions are experimental and have been inserted by the Minority Testing Fairness Coordinating Committee Council. They will not count against your score, but

I caution you to try your best on *all* questions, since you cannot be certain which they are. I presume you people know where to locate the lavatories, and for those of you fortunate enough not to be strapped by harried schedules so as to not necessitate wearing a timepiece, I shall display the hour on this green blackboard every fifteen minutes per each of the six sections. At the end of each section I shall say *Stop* and you shall all stop. If you are found to be still writing, you shall be asked to leave the test premises and your test will be invalidated. Finally, though we have laid down rubber matting, the gymnasium floor is slick, so be careful your chairs do not slip, or, in your own parlance—*Keep the four on the floor.* Is everything clear?

PRELIMINARY
SCHOLASTIC APTITUDE TEST

Test Booklet #dE101bR-H

NOTE: You MAY mark the test booklet, but these marks are NOT graded by the Educational Testing Service.

SECTION ONE (1): Verbal Relationships. Choose the words whose relationship most CLOSELY resembles the first cluster group conglomerate.

EXAMPLE:

MISCEGENATION: CRIME

a. black: beige
b. zebra: ape
c. Jane Russell: a sexy woman
d. jellyroll: gatemouth

The correct ANSWER is (c) because just as miscegenation used to be a crime, Jane Russell used to be a sexy woman.

Minutes: 20
Questions: 14

1. STRIKINGLY: GOOD-LOOKING
   a. cordially: invited
   b. thoroughly: enjoyed
   c. firmly: believed
   d. terribly: British

2. DEVOTED: FAN
   a. grueling: regime
   b. alarming: rate
   c. voracious: reader
   d. extolling: virtues

3. INSECURE: LOOSE
   a. piebald: apple tart
   b. sinecure: facial
   c. phonetics: turntable
   d. him: her

4. ANC: SAA
   a. TWA: CIA
   b. FCC: NRA
   c. FBI: AAA
   d. PBS: RPG

5. SPEISS: SPORAN
   a. tocher: toric
   b. exuviate: exoteric
   c. liberate: lixiviate
   d. blench: blowsy

6. RECEPTACLE: LOVEMAKING
   a. ephemeral: gauze
   b. quixotic: Spain
   c. firehose: Selma
   d. bulk mail: philately

7. NARRATIVE: PLATITUDES
   (a.) hot dog: shish kebab
   b. indict: corruption
   c. still life: montage
   d. monochromatic: piebald

8. CUTESY: WOOTSY
   a. boogie: woogie
   b. itsy: bitsy
   c. teeny: weeny
   d. artsy: fartsy

9. SLENDER: WAIST
   a. shapely: breasts
   b. knobby: knees
   c. broad: shoulders
   d. delicate: wrists

10. SCORCHING: SUN
   a. licking: flames
   b. howling: winds
   c. raging: clouds
   d. crashing: waves

11. MARTIAL: MARITAL
   a. siren: Siren
   (b.) fiend: friend
   c. enamored: enameled
   d. black: mail

12. CHOPHOUSE: GRILLROOM
   a. eatery: bistro
   b. misogyny: feminism
   c. brasserie: diner
   d. beanery: cookshack

13. BEBOP: MUZAK
   a. maverick: mule
   b. heretic: Jesuit
   c. amorphous: tenuous
   (d.) Coney Island: Great Adventure

14. MOUTH: GAPING
   a. grin: mischievous
   b. smile: radiant
   c. smirk: evil
   d. laugh: scornful

STOP!
End of Section One (1)
You may review THIS and ONLY THIS section.
DO NOT go on to the next section until told to do so.

SECTION TWO (2): Sentence-building. Choose the word that most CLOSELY fits the blank in the following sentence group clusters.

66

EXAMPLE:
The robust man _____ another guest wearing black Romanic leather sandals and fluorescent yellow socks who said, "But darling, Foucault was last year."
a. wheeled upon
b. whistled shrilly at
c. huffed, rolled his eyes toward
d. assaulted

The correct ANSWER is (c).
Minutes: 30
Questions: 17

1. The civil-rights leader was _____ to believe the police officer when he said he "liked the colored."
   (1) a. naïve
       b. insinuated
       c. onomatopoeia
       d. paid

2. The black boy knows that _____.
   (2) a. "Our top story tonight: The Van Camp's bean factory exploded this afternoon soon after their annual All-You-Can-Eat-What-A-Taste-Treat charity bean-a-thon. Fire inspectors call the blaze "suspicious."
       b. deep, deep, way down, we are all one and the same.
       c. it ain't the meat, it's the motion that makes your mama want to rock.
       d. yes, oh golly, yes! He would soon meet that special someone who would lead him not into temptation but deliver him into the wonderful world of hand-trembling, glass-shattering, adolescent lovemaking.

3. Though a boy of (3) _____ outward appearance, he knows that if the others understood how (4) _____ and (5) _____ he was, he would soon be loved by all.

(3) a. ebullient	(4) a. boring	(5) a. slipping
b. intravenous	b. vapid	b. just a smidgin
c. unremarkable	c. complicated	c. interesting, almost brilliant

d. piglike   d. interwoven   d. ribbed,
                                              colored,
                                              and
                                              scented
                                              for hours
                                              of added
                                              enjoy-
                                              ment

6. He often feels (6) _____ because of his perverse sexual urges, but at other times he thinks he is (7) _____ and just passing through the all-too-common rite of passage to manhood.

(6) a. soluble

    (b.) different, sick

    c. an intense desire to win and win big

    d. himself

(7) a. St. Zenobi, King of the Wild Frontier

    b. pretty as a picture

    (c.) hopelessly normal, re-placeable

    d. plátanos fritos

8. Though usually a man of his word, the homeroom teacher was less than honest when he said, "_____."

(8) a. *Ptou*

    b. Mama's baby, papa's . . .

    c. At Morgan's Chevrolet and Used Cars 'fidelity' is our middle name

    d. Janey's pregnant?

9. Opening his bedroom door _____, he was surprised to see a white nude Heimlich instructor giving his wife a lesson.

(9) a. quick as all get-out

    b. with the wind at his back and a good, stout ship under his feet

    c. flowers and chocolates in hand, after having made reservations for two at Windows on the World, chirping, "Happy anniversary, honey!"

    d. like a bat out of hell

10. The _____, the disillusionment with a movement that once filled him with such joyous and foolish optimism, is to what he attributes his current and unshakable cynicism.

(10) a. look of love

    b. aroma of fresh-baked taste treats

    c. pieces of the puzzle were finally coming together

    d. dream deferred once more

11. He _____ bumps into her in a public place just before the music swells and the camera CUTS to the tight close-ups of their faces revealing that dreamy surprise of finding that certain someone of your waking and sleeping dreams.
(11) a. unexpectedly
     b. perfunctorily
     c. knowingly
     d. always

12. The American commando (12) _____ leafs through *Mein Kampf* on a train lurching through war-torn and enemy-occupied France when (13) _____, a sinister-looking man in a black trench coat, a fedora pulled low over his bony face, small, round glasses, and an unshaven mug barks, "Your paperz! Your paperz! Rrrraus!"

(12) a. nonchalantly
     b. tepidly
     c. placidly
     d. tranquilly (yet inside he's a bundle of nerves)

(13) a. contusely
     b. ponderously
     c. suddenly
     d. not available in stores

14. "C'mon," said the rugged hero, clutching his Beretta in one hand, his woman in the other. "Let's get out of here!"
    They (14) _____ themselves through the passageway as Dr. Bülow's evil fortress shook mightily; rocks fell everywhere. Once outside, they dashed for their lives, he nearly flying her by her arm behind him like a kite when KA-BOOM! the fierce explosion dashed them to their feet. Moments later they (15) _____ rise to find just a charred, smoking hole where the mad, misguided doctor's laboratory once stood.

(14) a. rushed
     b. hurtled
     c. flung
     d. raced

(15) a. dazedly
     b. groggily
     c. wearily
     d. stunnedly

16. Even though the towering monster walked _____, and the girl was an Olympic silver-medalist miler, he caught her and began to strangle her at arm's length.
(16) a. slowly, arms akimbo
     b. ponderously, arms outstretched like a sleepwalker's
     c. like a regular live wire, a real wisenheimer
     d. lethargically, yet each mighty footfall quaked the earth

STOP!
End of Section Two (2)
You may review THIS and ONLY THIS section.
DO NOT go on to the next section until told to do so.

SECTION THREE (3): Reading Comprehension. Read the following passage snippet excerpts to come, then answer the questions based on a foundation grounded in what you have read.

EXAMPLE:
Most people do not know the interesting origins of Nabisco's Oreo cookie, one of the world's most-eaten dessert snack biscuits. If people realized that it was invented by a wealthy Afro-American baker and leader of the pro-assimilation movement of the 1940s, they might think twice before unscrewing the chocolate wafers and eating the cream filling separately.

The author probably believes that . . .
a. "Whitey is de devil."
b. Today is the first day of the rest of your life.
c. The already-troubled black bourgeoisie is now in danger of assimilating itself to smithereens.
d. The best things in life are free, me bucko, the best things in life are free.

The correct ANSWER is a matter of heated debate.
Minutes: 40
Questions: 12

One of the most charming and endearing of the many humorous anecdotes to come out of the civil-rights era concerns a certain Georgia church deacon, one of those fiery, uncompromising few who symbolized that struggle to make old Jim Crow take wing and fly from this Land of the Free.
(5)   It seems that his town's major department-store diners and restaurants continued to refuse to serve Afro-American customers, even though similar changes had already been made all over the South in the wake of the now-legendary boycotts and sit-ins. Well, that firebrand of a man, Deacon _____, took it upon himself to rally the hardworking Afro-American community to boycott every downtown store until they "changed their tune."

The town's level of tension was at an all-time high. The
(15) Deacon, who did not own an automobile himself, valiantly and
effectively organized those in the Afro-American community
with vehicles to drive the fifty miles to newly integrated Macon
to buy all their dry goods and sundries.

After two weeks of the boycott, the Deacon was called to
meet the town's Caucasian elders. Three hours later, the Deacon emerged and told his loyal and good-natured, trusting
flock, "Brethren, who wants to eat at their old smelly lunch
counters anyway? Shoot, I would not eat their old smelly food
even if you promised me a key to the gates o' heaven itself.
(25) Let us all go home and forget all this talk about boycotts. We
will fight them old white folks when it is really important."

And the funny end of the story came one month later, when
the stores *did* change their Jim Crow policy without seeming
to bow to Afro-American pressure, and that fiery stalwart, the
Deacon, won a brand-new, soft-blue Cadillac convertible in the
Chamber of Commerce's First Annual Negro Car Lottery!

1. The tone of the narrative is . . .
   a. jocular
   b. bitingly sarcastic
   c. caustic
   d. conversational

2. The Deacon is described as
   a. fiery
   b. corrupt
   c. valiant
   d. all of the above

3. The most precise title for this passage is
   a. Glory! One Chapter in the Struggle
   b. The Deacon's New Car
   c. Shameless: The Buying of Deacon _____
   d. Free at Last: "I Won't Be Takin' No Bus No Mo'!"

4. In line 17 "integrated" means
   a. your daughter can now marry anyone
   b. improved
   c. Afro-Americans have no more excuses
   d. all of the above

71

5. In line 22 the Deacon's speech is
   a. fake, contrived, as if written by a Northerner
   b. not even remotely believable, but brilliantly inciteful nevertheless
   (c.) wholly believable and effective, except that "key to the gates o' heaven" business
   d. good. I liked it very much

6. The anecdote itself is
   a. absolutely believable
   b. believable, but a bit overdone, especially the end
   c. true, trust me, I'll even tell you his real name if you want
   (d.) true, but not such a big deal as the author would have us believe. After all, they did get what they wanted

"We are both of us so rich and possessing such impossibly good looks, let us make love like a proud stallion and a mare, or perhaps like two Greek statues newly come to life," husked Wayne as he sipped his Moët in his 150-foot yacht bound for
(5) Portofino.

"Zere's nothing Greek about what we're going to do, *mon cher*," chortled Monique as she let slip her diamond-sequined ball gown, revealing two perfect globes of lust, then stepped into the life raft filled with caviar and thusly concealed her neatly trimmed, keystone copse.

He untied his Giorgio Armani black-silk bow tie and tossed it into the churning wake of the expensive ship, then disrobed from his Pierre Cardin double-breasted tuxedo and threw the entire suit into the sea, leaving himself naked save for the silk,
(15) custom-made shoulder holster cuddling his Beretta 48C he had nicknamed "Sinbad."

"Zon't zou zare throw my gown overboard, bee-cauze iz ze ony clothz I bring," throated the naked Frenchwoman.

Wayne picked up her Yves Saint-Laurent original, the sequins twinkling in the moonlight, and unceremoniously balled it up. "Neither of us will be needing any clothing on this trip," he cooed deeply as he pitched the shimmering frock into the turbulent waves, which made him recall his rough-and-tumble childhood bouncing from foster home to reform schools, mak-
(25) ing friends only by being the best sandlot pitcher and hardest hitter in all of West Philly.

"*C'est la vie, mais* come on zin, ze *l'eau* iz fine," nasaled Monique sexily as she splashed herself with the Russian beluga, then fingered some caviar off her proud and jutting pencil erasers and licked her fingers clean.

"In a minute, froggy," gruffed Wayne as he donned his wet suit and scuba gear. "I've got an illegal underwater plutonium-mining operation to blow up."

7. Monique is
   a. a tease
   b. Mata Hari
   c. a whale of a gal
   d. typical

8. If Monique had succeeded in luring Wayne into the caviar bath,
   a. *he* would have stealthily disconnected *his* twin pros-thetic breasts and deeply growled, "Secret agent man, the jig is up. Did you forget I, your evil nemesis, Dr. Zamboni's thick calves so soon?"
   b. she would have made love with him wildly, then tried to sever his brain stem with a hairpin just as he gruffly grabbed her wrist, made her cry, and spilled the beans.
   c. she would have looped her arms around his neck and kissed him softly, then pulled him gently on top of her, arched her muscular, smooth, tanned back, and guided him gently into her valley of the shadow of Love.
   d. she would have run her arms over his rippling biceps sprinkled with scratches and scars and asked where each wound came from, then kissed each scarred arm, then his chest, his stomach, and down and down, until he would no longer remember his name, nor would he care.

9. How many times has "globes of lust" (line 8) appeared in print?
   a. just this once
   b. twice
   c. in *Squirt* magazine alone, 3.5×10^4 (as of 3/1/84)
   d. more times than I care to remember, thank you

10. How did Wayne get so wealthy if he grew up in foster homes and reform schools? (line 24)

a. One day, a large yacht moored on the lake near his last juvenile hall. He stowed away on the vessel, and when he was discovered, the yacht's owner so admired his chutzpah, he adopted him.

b. He was a hustling and scamming ragamuffin, stole when he had to, extorted when the need arose, amassed a large fortune eventually, but when the Internal Revenue Service caught wind of his little scam and was hot on his trail, they offered him one last out: "Work for us," they said, "and you won't go to the hoosegow."

c. Attending Stanford University on a basketball scholarship, his gregarious nature and winning good looks soon earned him a berth in the easy elitism of the school's fraternity system. Through these contacts, he met and married a meat-packing mogul's homely daughter, Megan Winston, who wound up the victim of a tragic gangland slaying.

d. A good-looking boy of fourteen, he would mow lawns of the mansions on the other side of the tracks. One day, a wealthy divorcée paid him $100, saying, "I've got a lawn to mow inside too." (Repeat)

The good, homely folk of Lowndes County never expected they would ever get a gander of the likes of this here. Little Eehssi Robinson, Pernice's baby daughter, burning down Route 69 in a brand-new, shiny red foreign number, coming in even faster
(5) than she had fled their quaintproudnoblesimplejoyousglorious-triumphalnice hamlet ten years before to attend university. They all knew she was living in California; probably in one of those big, fancy old houses up on those hills they'd seen in the moving pictures every Sunday, and she'd become right famous and won prizes, and her books were in the library and all, but no one, not even the boozy preacherman, expected such a shiny red sports car.

So there they were, the whole town out on their clean-smelling front stoops watching that shiny red streak and the
(15) plume of dust that followed close behind like Ham's ghost. The streak and that ghost—that brown cloud of memory—finally slowed down to brave the cratered drive up to the house from where the writer was birthed.

"He-llo, Ma-ma," enunciated the jubilant writer. "I am absolutely fatigued after such a long journey . . . Oh, and, Mama, 'fatigued' means tired."

Mama, her nostrils proudly flaring like a holy god's chariot-pulling mare, her heavy, joyous bosom rising and falling with every profound breath of that sweet Georgia wind, her legs as (25) strong and as stout as the mighty Georgia pines, exuberantly hoisted that heavy iron skillet high over her kerchief-covered head, the skillet from which she had fried the eggs and bacon and ham and apples and cornbread, and had cooked the grits and greens and black-eyes and chit'lin's and okra for her thirty healthy children, and she swung that skillet down with a quickness far beyond her seventy years onto the hot-combed hair of her youngest daughter, Eehssi, killing the child with a *clonk.*

" 'Fatigued,' my ass."

11. How would you describe the style of this passage?
    a. neoclassical
    b. postmodern
    ⓒ Afro-Baroque
    d. mock Afro-Baroque

12. If Eehssi had not said, " 'Fatigued' means tired" (line 21), how would the story have ended?
    a. Little had changed in her sleepy little hamlet. Where she had expected envy and ignorance, she found instead a spirituality that had been missing from her life ever since she had left. It was precisely at this moment that she decided to return—not once a decade as she had previously done—but every summer; not for the people, not even for Mama, but for her own now-blossoming soul.
    b. The sun was warmer here, the air sweeter, and the smiles so much broader, and it was then and only then that Eehssi could not remember why it was she had ever left.
    c. "Welcome home, child," said Mama quietly. Eehssi glowed. Somewhere in the distance, watchful hounds barked. They too welcomed her home.
    ⓓ An old turkey buzzard circled aimlessly in the endlessly blue sky as the smell of cooking molasses—the best smell in the whole wide world, she thought

to herself—tickled her nostrils with sweet, deliciously sweet memories of a little pigtailed girl with honey knees and ashy elbows who one day said to no one in particular, "I-am going to be-a writer."

STOP!

End of Section Three (3)
You may review THIS and ONLY THIS section.
DO NOT go on to the next section until told to do so.

22

C'mon, you losers, let's go hang out at Las Palabras Doradas and I'll tell you all the ones you missed, says Andy, but Donald grabs Andy's arm and Earle jabs him with a knuckle fist, because there is this spot they say that if you hit just right on the arm they get an instant charley horse and their whole arm is temporarily paralyzed for a while (even though it never really works). Anyway, Earle says he knows this great place up on One Twenty-fifth Street and Lenox Avenue where the lady there won't probably charge, she likes him so much. He fixed her toaster—there was just a screw loose—but Andy says no way, he'd get knifed even before he got off the train, and Donald says the same thing, only *he* could probably pass and get away with it, his mother being black and all, but only if he didn't act like such a frigging goombah. So finally Earle says it's an adventure, so he is going anyway, with or without those wussies.

MON.
Wake up by 7:00!!!
PSAT!!!

Harlem Adventure? (Daughter?)
Tape L.G.*2–4am

he had written on an already-claimed Chinese hand-laundry ticket on the bus coming home from the movie last night. Now his left hand's fingers curve over this Do-list lying on his thigh, protecting it from unwanted gazes.

The first out the subway door, Earle walks to the northwest subway exit and up each stair. As he rises to the level of the street, the many little yellow light bulbs in her window spelling Chez Darcelle blink and hum into his eyes and ears.

Oh my Lord! Look who walks into my door. It's my favorite toaster repairman. Child, you just have a seat. Anywhere you want. Earle looks down, then quickly sits on the closest stool.

The usual, please, he orders. Darcelle squints at him, scratches her head with her right index finger, looks at the ceiling, then she smiles and shouts:

BISCUIT AND VISCERA, WET AND FAT.

Now Earle smiles as he sees the velvet blacklite painting of Martin, John, and Robert on the wall, the scenic calendar from Jewelle's Showplace of Beauty, the old man at the counter looped over his coffee like a vulture. *The fact that I chose to come here to this strange and dangerous place proves how special I really am.* The chicken livers and biscuits and grits and gravy arrive steaming, along with a large root beer, on the house.

With Darcelle angled over a table, her wide butt swaying to counterbalance her dishrag rubs on the Formica, Dorothy twists the knob at the base of the clock—too far—then quickly twists it back a bit to point the hands to one o'clock exactly. She fast-

*Love Girls, on Showtime After Hours

taps the glass even after her mother is unlocking the cashier booth door. Dorothy presses the door and Darcelle away and runs into

Excuse m/Hey, watch eh/What? I'm sorr/What?/I apologi/
You should apol/I'm sor/Enough already, just don/
Wait/Wait, you go fir/No/No/No, talk/After you/sorr/
Will you quit/Sorry/This isn't work/I'll shut/What?/
Nothi/Is silly/Yeah, let's start/Again. Okay. What's
your name?/Earle/Dorothy/Dorothy? No, Earle/*My* name/
Oh! I get/*Dorothy*/it. And I'm Earle./You're Earle.
Well, goodbye, Earle, I'm late. This lady here will
take your bill.

23

What a black foxy babe! She's only the prettiest black chick I've ever seen and the last time up there I didn't even see a one that grabbed me. Wow I bet she dances, the way she stands so straight and she's no dummy or junkie or nothing you could tell by the way she talked, her mom was right she is wild just the way I like em (heh heh). Talked? What a goombah stu-nod you are talking over her like a parrot and besides running into her like Ray Charles or something she probably hates you for that but what if she doesn't? Earle stop it, don't get your hopes up because something always happens remember Janey (Oh I'm sure she wants me guys 'cause once at assembly she took off her shoes and crossed her legs so her foot was leaning right into my pants and she didn't move it for at least a minute) and you thought you'd go off like Old Faithful right there while Mister Wyte was introducing the renowned Joe Schmoe Wind Ensemble but no more of that, but what if Dorothy—what if she wants you? Who

knows why but love is blind I hope to God because then I've got a
chance, geez it's been so long since I've seen some pretty girl I didn't
want to just bone right there in the downtown train and man, Dorothy,
I'd die just to kiss her wouldn't even stick it in even if she paid me,
even if she begged like those Hustler *douchebags but she wouldn't*
that's for sure. And another thing, even though she's Ay number-one
fantasy fuel I'll never schwang the wonker over her picture. Bad luck,
and Janey proves it, and to tell you the truth I didn't even notice her
breasts or butt or nothing I couldn't tell you what her bod's like if you
paid me, but I bet it's fanfuckintastic that's for sure and that's another
thing, Operation Dorothy, I'm going up there all the time and dress
well and not even do it at all until at least after our first date or for
this whole month, whichever comes first. Crap! You passed the fuckin
stop Mr. Potatohead, geez . . .

November 30, 1984

To Whom It May Concern:

Are you so blindly enthralled with that postmodernist, semi-
ological sophism (that incidentally *nobody* believes in anymore)
that the words "narrative" and "continuity" mean nothing to
you? Have you never read Baldwin?

Your transparent jealousy of my oft-praised literary successes
is truly pathetic to behold. I receive so many vitriolic letters
from countless other underachieving middle-aged black male
"artists" who cannot bear to watch a sister trade in *your* feeble
slaps and drunken sexual abuse for American Book Awards
and tenured chairs at Princeton. I feel for you, sir, but only
enough to beg you to heed my heartfelt advice: For God's
sake . . . LEARN A TRADE!!!!!!

Isshee Ayam

P.S. Don't think I didn't catch that childish barb about the
(multi) award-winning, San Francisco–based writer and her
mother's frying pan. Grow up.

Miss Johnson handed Earle a copy of Paul Lawrence Dunbar's poetry, and to Dorothy, Phillis Wheatley's, and asked the new female scholar to erase that grand slate blackboard, blacker even than the face of old "Afro Joe," a man more ancient than dirt, they said, born in that ever-calling, mystical continent—Africa—in a place he still calls Joruba.

Earle skipped out of that stout little school happier, more fulfilled, than he had been in years. Whistling down the long, dusty road of tears and sweat, he remembered the surge of joy that swelled within him when he read that erstwhile mystical passage, a swell he had never before known, yet a swell quickly eclipsed by an even more powerful surge of feelings and thoughts and answered prayers—brought on by Dorothy. Earle began to whistle joyously in tune with the rush of the wind through the tall, swaying fingers of the mighty Georgia oaks and the gentle babble of Sinner's Creek, which ran alongside the proud dirt road—inseparable lovers, yet so very, very different.

At the creek's edge stood Cornbread and Bassmouth.

"Wail, wail, wail. Looka what we gots here," sarcasmed Bassmouth. "We gots oursef a boy too big fer his britches."

"Yeah, Mr. Brainy," whined Cornbread. "You shouldn't be goin' round makin' yo friends look stupid."

Earle's newly opened, cleaned, and refreshed eyes stared not at his two sexist former friends. Instead, he fixed his ever growing and expanding stare on an as yet nonexistent point up ahead—his bright and shining future—and kept on keeping on. He held his head high with a pride the other two would never know, even if they had not later been dismembered by the Nazi war machine.

Bassmouth ran up to the changed Earle and grabbed his shoulders, pushed the neo-nascent scholar down to the dust of the earth, and Earle groaned and made a tight, almost white-knuckled fist of pure rage, when that new, hardly explicable force once again welled from within and suddenly and utterly calmed him. Earle rose. Yet again Bassmouth slammed him down, our proud boy now spitting gritty dirt and rich red blood from that mouth from which—only moments earlier—flowed such a lovely fountain of rich words. Again Earle rose.

"C'mon, Bassmouth, let's leave that old smelly Earle to his own mis'ry," whined Cornbread, tugging at the big-muscled arms of Bassmouth, who merely shrugged the restraint away.

"Make us look bad," he barked, punching Earle's chest hard. "This'll teach yuh not ta go 'head make monkey out yo friends jus' ta make de sweet-eye on no ugly yeller bitch." Now Bassmouth let loose a torrent of fists, soon forcing our proud young intellectual into a hunched ball.

"Stop, you stupid, strong bully!" yelled Dorothy as she kicked Bassmouth squarely in his prostate, making him slump to the ground and clasp his defined groin.

Dorothy was Earle's crutch as he limped down the road.

CHAPTER **SIX** **A SPECIAL WOMAN**

"Your friends have a strange way of showing how much they care." Dorothy's mother, Darcelle, smiled as she daubed his wounds with a cloth moistened by the cool water in a bowl held by Dorothy's concerned and slightly trembling hands.

"Thank you, ma'am, for dressin' my cuts and all," strained Earle. "I think I'll be going home now." Earle coughed and grimaced as he tried to raise his battered head, then fell back onto a pillow, ran his tongue over his tender teeth, and extracted a bloody molar.

"You just remain there in bed," soothed Darcelle. "I have already sent a boy to tell your mother where you are. You just get some rest now, you hear?"

"One more thing, ma'am," hoarsed Earle as his weary eyes neared closing. "How come you learn to talk so good-well, if youse from the country like we is?" Yet Earle could not remain conscious for the heady answer in the wake of the day's many excitements. He was soon snoring deeply.

Back in the spring of 1919, the smart, pretty seventeen-year-old was the pride of Macon County, so it came as no surprise to that luminously vibrant sharecropping community when Darcelle Lamont won a full scholarship to Spelman College in Atlanta. The preacher shined his worn buckboard and cleaned his horses to take her to college himself, and Big Jake, the town's kindhearted carpenter and smithy, made her a large trunk of stout oak and loaded it himself onto the back of the buggy. All the Afro-Americans in the county lined Main Street, weeping with joy to see their collective daughter drive off to the "Paris of the South"—to education, knowledge, and, most of all, to hope.

Once at school, she studied harder than most and was soon regarded as one of the brightest students in all of Atlanta. Everyone assumed she would make a fine and honorable teacher—even up North, if she so desired.

Then it happened. Not unlike many young female students of any decade, Darcelle became especially close to one particular professor. He was witty and charming and intelligent and so strong—and white. Though many of the professors at the all-Afro-American, all-female college were white Quaker males, none but Professor A— seemed so completely without derision or condescension for his students' race. He brought such a semblance of care and warmth to his literature lectures that it is understandable indeed how he could make an impressionable, bright, and pretty young country girl fall so very hopelessly in love.

Darcelle will always remember the day she entered his spacious office with its illustrations by Blake on the walls and that large, very soft leather couch. Her pigtails flounced as she walked, and one knee sock refused to stand tall and protect her shapely young calf, but she was determined to ask Professor A— what Marvell meant when he penned, "Had we but world enough and time,/ This coyness, lady, were no crime." Yet perhaps, in her heart of hearts, she already knew.

"Do come in, um, Miss Lamont, isn't it?" intoned the professor, his handsome gray temples flexing with every movement of his jaw.

Yes, she came in and sat in that office she would soon know all too well. She entered and discussed love poetry, poetry, love, all while their eyes unashamedly probed each other's, each thinking, Could they possibly want me as much as I want, I need, them? But each also knowing the impossibility of their wants. On one occasion, at the door, ready to leave, Darcelle knew that if she turned back toward the room, she would be lost forever; if she looked ahead and left, she would be forever safe, yet hollow. Hollow. She turned back quickly and leaped into his outstretched arms.

He locked the door and guided her to that couch. That couch! And they each disrobed, slowly, tenderly. Never had she seen a white man nude, and her little brother was the only Afro-American male she had ever seen without raiment. She tried to breathe quietly and not shake with fear, but honestly, if the room had exploded and had the Almighty Himself appeared, she would not have felt emotions more strong than those now so urgently tugging her down.

The first time it was inside her was pain and blood and mainly fear; the fiftieth time was hours of kisses and caresses, licks and sucks, rich, pungent, earthy, wet smells and loud grunts and pants, clawing and praying and whimpers and whoops and spasm after spasm after spasm—even now the mere remembrance brought a rich surging flush to her cheeks and to her thighs.

But there was no fifty-first time. When she told him she was pregnant, he told her he was married.

Expelled from school, she wandered the South with her little daughter, thankfully dark enough to quell too many questions. To feed young Dorothy, Darcelle would iron and wash for the rich whites in town, and when gentle, little, innocent Dorothy was still unshod as winter fast approached, Darcelle would sob as she relit the red lamp on her porch and work until the town's womenfolk threw rocks at her shack or tried to spit at her child. Long before, she had wired Macon telling them their bright, young Darcelle had died.

That next clear, joyous morning, Earle opened his sandy eyes to a beaming Dorothy. He felt a warmth on his hand, a fulfilling, human warmth. It was Dorothy's hand.

"How did you sleep," asked the concerned girl as she hurriedly removed her flesh from his.

"None too good, but better I reckon than I woulda if it weren't for you kind folks," he uttered sprightly. "And thank ye for kicking old Bassmouth, but I swear I never thought I'd see the day that a girl goes and saves my life."

"We womenfolk can do a whole bunch of things when we put our minds to it, Mr. Pride, I'll have you know," she huffed. "Now go get dressed. We got school."

"Funny," he began. "I don't remember gettin' outta my clothes."

Dorothy exited, closing the stout oaken door behind her with a solid *clonk* and a hot blush.

24

Earle! What took you so long? The PeeEssAyTee was over hours ago. Julie, Donald's mother, and Mrs. Williams said that Donald and Andy were already home. I swear you just about put me in my grave, you scared me so . . .

I'm going to the hairdresser's, then straight from there I'm going out tonight, but there's a chicken in the oven that will be done around six and there's rice pilaf mix in the cupboard and of course peas and corn and things in cans; oh, and I found some old fudge swirl in the back of the freezer that needs to be eaten before it goes bad, but smell it first just to make sure . . .

How do I look? Not my hair, of course, but everything else? I'll call around ten to make sure everything's all right, but if there's an emergency, you can always call Donald's mother. Don't stay up too late, Handsome Harry . . .

25

Earle reads an article on desert warfare in *Merchant of Death: The Mercenaries' Monthly* until his dinner is ready, then reclines in the Stratolounger, the chicken on a plate in his lap, the television remote control unsteady on the armchair's arm, and a root beer at his feet. The television ignites with a ZWOOM and a crackle of static and much too large a volume of noise. Snatching the remote control, Earle sprays the twenty-seven-inch UltraColorMatic with the infrared beam that commands the set to quiet itself. He then changes the beam's wavelength to the ScanTron-Plus mode and the appliance begins its automatic ten-second channel sampler:

Gosh, she's the most beautiful woman I've ever seen: sexy, sweet, witty, and intelligent too, but what's this? Oh no, she's scratching her head. Must be dandruff. Forget—

If Lucy didn't realize Ricky hid the gunpowder from the fire-crackers he took away from Little Ricky in the pepper shaker, then that means at the ladies' club luncheon, Lucy's *Boeuf Flambé*—

Fire and Ice is like no other synthetic motor oil on the market today, since it is fortified with Polyaminide-80, so will protect your car in an extra-special way far too complicated to explain here on Tee—

"Visionary" is how I'd describe myself, Merv. Know that sounds conceited, what have you, but I feel darn proud to be the first celebrity of note to have his own line of designer Lucite furniture—

"We're movin' on up/to the East Side/to a dee-luxe apartment in the sky-ayyy./Aw movin' on up/to the East Side./We fin'ly got a piece of the pie"—

Aaaaaaaay! Tonight at eight o'clock you have an appointment with terror. From the director who brought you such classics as *Bloodbath* and *Eyeballs* comes—

The bride's name is Coco and the groom, a Mr. Pinky. [Laughs.] No, they're not hippies or members of some cult group, but rare Rwandan mountain gorillas, and zoo officials are hoping the two—

Suspects, both black males, ages twenty to thirty-five, one of stocky build wearing a gold chain that says *Classy Dude*—

. . . is the title track of his latest album . . . Good news for all you Bill DePopulaire fans. His new "Love" video will be comin' atchou in about ten minutes, so stay tuned for—

No! If Chrissie doesn't know she mistook her overnight bag for the traveling contraceptive salesman's identical valise, then that means while she's away at the religious retreat with the priests and nuns and—

Mr. Maplewood! [scream the boys and girls after pulling off

his ghost mask]. Yes, it's me. And I would have succeeded if it weren't for you meddling kids—

. . . about all the time we've got for today, but be sure and tune in tomorrow, when our guests will be Charles Nelson Reilly, Brett and Elke Sommers, Henry Gibson—

:TeeVee has-beens and never wases. *Bing!* [applause]. Yachts, skiing in St. Moritz, fur aerobic apparel, chauffeurs, caviar baths, Moët, island homes, Fortune 500—

. . . degree days for the month of May. And for tomorrow, Accu-Weather's SkyCam shows we can expect some scattered showers throughout the day. Of course, I'll have an up-to-the-minute update and five-day forecast at eleven o'—

No! If Bitsy didn't realize Jim hid the hashish he had confiscated from Muffin in the herbal tea tin, then that means for Bitsy's tea party with her mother-in-law—

. . . and order now! Rush $9.95 for this extra-special burglar alarm, smoke and noxious-fume detector, and emergency lighting system, because remember: if you knew when calamity would strike—

. . . no balls, top of the eighth, Reds 2, Yanks 8. And here comes Cranky Robinson to the mound, the newest member of the Yankee organization, and—

Real cheese, real milk, real potatoes, real herbs and spices, that's why Swiney's Au Gratin Potato Food is America's favorite and a special—

. . . guest today, the spokesperson for all the black people in this country, the Right Reverend Ms. Swoosy Ayomie. And of course the lovely and vivacious Tata will be joining us later on—

. . . in the birthplace of the egg and the most delicate of woman's magical and beautiful reproductive organs—

. . . and Moog synthesizer, Art Blakey on drums, Wynton Marsalis trumpet and cornet, Branford Marsalis tenor sax, Joe Pass guitar, Milt Jackson vibes. Coltrane's "My Favorite Things"—

. . . toys or flashlights all need reliable high-energy batteries and there's really only one choice. So if any of these small appliances could talk, they'd say—

I can talk! I CAN TALK! Oh, thank you so much, Doctor, for forcing me to come back to the very spot where my family was blown up and slapping me hard, because right after the orchestral epiphany I blinked and opened my mouth and am again a normal and desirable young wo—

No! If Slide ain't knowed Smurf done hid dat industrial-strength laxative in dat milk bottle so his 'rents won't know he sick after stayin' out late eatin' Meskin, den dat means Slide, during de middle of de basketball champeenship—

The oil on *your* tankers? You must be insane, Prince Fa'had. The only way Karrington Co.'d do business with the likes of your ilk is over my dead body—

. . . and breath odor? When your problem is *everybody's* problem, reach for Discreet with Actizol, and raise your arms high. So discover—

We've hidden a camera and microphone in this famous department store's ladies' dressing room. Let's hear what these women have to say about cotton—

No, but it is cottony soft, so if you love your children and don't want some social agency to take them away, you'll spend the extra pennies for *their* bottoms—

Up men, 'cause that's the last of the water. Rizzuto, Razcinsky, Ryan, Robinson, we're gonna try to take that hill, but we'll probably just end up chopped meat on the wrong end of a Commie Chinese's bayonet. Move!—

Out! What a play! Let's see that again in super slow mo . . . So final score, eight to three and from all of us here at Double-you Pee Eye Ex Sports, thank you and good night, and since we went a little over, time-wise, we'll switch right to our *Six O'Clock Springtime Special*. This week, a nineteen sixty-two Nat King Cole

Earle's mother's
apartment on the
Upper West Side,
Manhattan.

St. Rita's School
for Girls,
side entrance.

Mr. Morgan's
homeroom, Friends
Academy.

Coney Island.

Coney Island.

Darcelle Pride's apartment in Harlem.

Interior of the restaurant Picaresque on the Upper West Side, Manhattan.

Barnard College.

Christmas Extravaganza already in progress/"And though it's been said many times, many ways, Merry Christmas to you."

26

All garbage, says Earle. He taps the remote control to pop the screen to a shrinking, glowing nebula crackling static.

The apartment is completely dark and nearly quiet. Jets and ambulances must be shouting and screaming outside, but inside, the wooden floor's little pops and the refrigerator's *mmmmm* control. By not pushing up the light switch (On), Earle practices blindness. He toes the floor, fingers the air high and low around his face. Somewhere soon will come the dining-room table, a serving tray on wheels, then the door of his mother's room. He overcautiously believes the table is closer than it is so reaches many feet before being an arm away from its hard corners.

Kicking the serving tray, the decanters upon it gossip but don't break. The dim reflection of the dark in the glass over the Impressionist print next to his mother's door fools him. He steps into the shimmer and stings his nose.

Left of her dark doorway, reaching inside, Earle wipes the wall again and again, but does not touch the light switch. He enters and faces the wall and pushes his hand through the area. Always where he had already checked twice, he feels the switch's nub and so gently eases it up. The slowness mutes the usual brittle click. He is a spy looking for the secret Nazi papers in this, the swanky apartment of an important Nazi's girlfriend. Even at his age.

Pushing up a mattress corner, he slides his hand over the boxspring. Nothing. He lowers the mattress and smooths the blankets, but not too much, for they were not perfect before. In the nightstand drawer, not one interesting thing: knickknacks, tchotchkes gewgaws, bric-a-brac. From the top dresser drawer, the sour panties' smell escapes and pools thick behind his nose. Sperm smell does the same. In the back of the drawer he finds it. A small plastic case. The giant rubber microdot nests inside. Near it, the tube of decoding foam.

Why didn't she take this gunk with her if she was going out on a date? She probably has another set and just leaves this around to make me think she doesn't pork.

Earle is looking for something else when he sees his father's records above the wall unit. His mother smiles and holds him whenever she hears the old sounds.

He fingers out the corner, then pinches and pulls Coltrane's *The Atlantic Years* from the stack. He pulls the album cover from around the dust jacket, then the jacket from around the record— holding the edges lightly as he remembers being taught by him. Now clumsily elbowing up the turntable's dustcover, he circles the album's center over the spindle until the hole finds the spike.

"My Favorite Things" begins with conventional Sounds of Music: a pretty ditty just long enough to lull for keyboard and sax—saxophone and pianoforte fall/fly thru Beat-improvised shrieks whistles blasts of pain love humor, no logic not one expected note just soundZ that attack fondle hurt tickle embrace pinch without end takin' care of Jack wacky demons it seems against efficiency reason the Tried trite probable (and True?) jumps clicks switches erratic as electron erratic because hEiseNBerg say don't know exactly where it is ever becauz you're *looking* changes (it) but how you know if you don't look? only ColtraneTyner even more K-razy 'cause Heisy guesses electron is in cloud P2 but *no*body guesses where notes is at until they is *at* already. Then they land again, the two do, all safe, secure, and Sound, and already known. The famous melody is an outline in everyone's brain, and we just watch to see what new colors (if any) the cats will use to fill in the sketch to make our comfortable memory breathe a bit, then whooPS! there they go again with crashwhooping through Mach II $\times$ 10^8 we happy just hold on don't crash like new world not safe but flood pumping churning butter 'n' blood you'd not blink now if record explode head pop roof saint/bum talkin' tongues brand-new day snap cracklepop, snap cracklepop, snap cracklepop, snap cracklepop, snap cracklepop, snap cracklepop, snap cracklepop, snap cracklepopzzzzzzzzzzzzzzcwoopts

You must be a friggin' wacko 'cause you feel just like that.

27

Every Monday afternoon Dorothy and her three friends from St. Rita's strut out the school's imposing and ornate gothic gates still wearing their short plaid school kilts. As they gossip, they each poke the air with their cigarettes, ignoring the stares of men.

Around the corner, out of sight, they must now be climbing the stairs.

Opening the door at the stairs' top on whose bumpy glass is painted ACCADEMIA AMERICANA DELLA FRANCESCA MONTOVANI, Dorothy sees what she always sees. The adults in their four rows of "Aerobics for the Obese" fold toward her, then rotate and reach at the tall windows.

Dorothy points her finger at each of the shapes, her thumb straight up in the air. Pow. Pow. Pow, she is seen to whisper.

Excellent, *ciccioni* [clapclap], but *basta* for today. Now I titch the pretty *ragazze* . . . *Forza*, my little girls, too much work this day.

Her back now to the kind window, Signora Montovani supervises the girls' undressing.

Ragazze! [clapclap] You stay farr frrom window if you do not want bus drrivers to see your *poppe*.

Topless and multiplied by the wall mirrors, the young ladies peg their hair, step into their leotards, unroll them over their contours, stretch one sleeve over a hand, wrists, elbow, stretch over a shoulder, and release (snapsnapsnapapap). Then the other side. *Pronto, signora!*

They stretch (*ed uno e due*) on the bar (*e tre e quattro*), legs so lithe and shapely, toes so sweet and grape, arms waft down and out and up and down, through a mist of foggy lense/Buttocks twitch and twist in circled world of superzoom/Faces smile no more but introspect on girlish things . . .

After class, tights roll off their bodies as sweat shines off their bodies everywhere. Now covering their legs with jeans that stop at the calf and their feet with colorful pumps, their blouses, now untucked, hang low and adorably oversized. They push the tops of nozzles that blast them with body spray, and leave.

Dorothy and her three friends step down the sidewalk, arms hooked together, their black-string, left-ankle bracelets dance. Their combined width sweeps oncoming pedestrians into the street. At the rosy, marbled columns and brass track lighting and hanging plants under the neon cursive *Picaresque*, Olivia ceremoniously swings back the mahogany and smoked-glass door to usher in Julie, Dorothy, and Sheena.

28

They make their grand entrance and look all around for the spot with the best-looking guys. But you can't really go wrong at Picaresque, because it is like always filled to the brim with *gorgeous* male specimens and not Friends or Collegiate or Trinity or Carver boys either, but real hot diplo-preps during break and Columbia biz or med studs and even actors and models, but of course there's always also the fat, middle-aged bee-men scamming to screw around behind their Scarsdale wives' backs with a girl old enough to be his daughter and real close to jailbait in the city, and *absolutely* jailbait in New Jersey and Connecticut. Anyway, Yassir, he's Lebanese but nice, owns the place and is pretty hot-looking, dark and swarmy, but a real live letch but gives them drinks for free, because he wants pretty girls in the place. So he comes up and *oohs* and *aahs* and talks about how they are like the four most beautiful princesses in the city, and he hugs them all and gives them kisses on both cheeks, like Europeans, and seats them in the window. He smells real hot, says Olivia, and Dorothy says, You should know, because Olivia fools around with him once in a while. They're not going out or anything, it's just like pure lust. Olivia smiles and looks around to see if no one's looking, then holds her hands out like a foot apart, because she says he's like gorgeous and big, and the other girls laugh and look at his pants, and she must be right, says Sheena, or he's got a fresh-pepper grinder down there. Julie pretends to get up and says, I'll go find out, but Olivia grabs her wrist and says he's off limits, only half-joking, because Julie is really sweet and all but she's also great-looking—blond hair, half-French, half-Israeli, and has this nasty habit of sleeping with her best friend's boyfriends.

The waiter comes up and asks if they would care for dinner, but Dorothy says, Just drinks, strongly, like daring him to ask for EyeDees, because if they ever got carded here that'd be it, 'cause they'd have Yassir can the guy on his butt like that (snap). Of course they all order Pina Coladas, and of course Sheena says *Piña* like a Mexican, to remind them all that she went to Mazatlán for Easter and still has the tan lines to prove it. She's black but real light-skinned and very pretty, even if her thighs thunder a bit, but the guys don't care, because they're always on her case like flies. Her dad is like the biggest real-estate developer on the Island and they've been written about in *Ebony* and their house in Sag is absolutely gorgeous, but Sheena pretty much lives on her own in her folks' hot apartment on East Eighty-sixth, because of school and all, so her place is like where they all crash after a night of clubbing. They usually stay up until Spazio closes— around four or five—then get breakfast at the Empire and call it quits.

Anyway, in the corner are four guys, and of course they're checking them out, and of course the girls pretend not to see, act all cool and whatnot while they say, Don' turn around! Three of them are hunks, one's oh kay, I get the blond, he's sooooo cute, I know the one in chinos, he used to go to Andover with my brother, but now I think he's a Ford model, he's soo hot, maybe they'll take us to Chic?

Then the one in the chinos gets up and walks over to the girls, asking if he could interrupt their conversation, ladies? and Dorothy looks up at him real bored-like and shrugs her shoulders. My name is Richard Manilow and my friends and I could not help noticing, ah, excuse me, you are? he asks at Dorothy. Dorothy, she says real flatly, but he takes her hand anyway and kisses it lightly, looking down her arm to her eyes, and he opens his gorgeous green eyes wide. He does the same for Olivia, Sheena, and Julie, and all four girls play dead, like a Ford model kisses their hands every day. Would you care to join us? he asks, pointing to his friends. The girls look at each other and are all practically yawning, they are acting so good, well, and Dorothy scrunches her shoulders and says, Why not, and Richard escorts her to his table, where his friends all stand up and kiss hands and stuff, then work it so every girl is next to a guy, but Julie gets stuck with the one that's almost bald, his hair is so thin, and you can just tell Olivia and Sheena are a bit afraid she'll try and horn in on theirs. But even Julie wouldn't dare go after Dorothy's, because it's obvious Richard was aiming for her from the start, and besides, Dorothy would absolutely mutilate her.

So, ladies, what do you all do? asks one of the boys in a Kenzo shirt that must have cost a mint.

We go to Smith, but next year we're all going to transfer to Stanford because Smith is seriously dead, says Dorothy, who's used that one before, so the other girls can't be too surprised, and Julie says that yeah, Northampton is just wall-to-wall students, with Smith and You-Mass and Holyoke (yech!) and Amherst, because her brother goes to Amherst, so she knows all about that stuff.

Richard says that the Coast is really great, they'll like Stanford. When he did the Eye. Magnin Fall/Winter catalogue last year, they flew him out. And Sheena's says he's got a lot of friends out there, they all say they love it, so Sheena asks hers where he goes and he says Columbia Med, but it's just his first year. He just escaped from Yale (laughs). Yale? says Julie, leaning over her guy and Sheena. Did he know Winslow Pepper? and of course the guy says back, Winnie? They did Saybrook together. He's good people, and Julie explains how he dated a friend of hers, and goes on and on, until she catches Sheena's real dirty look.

Richard asks if anybody's hungry, because he's got to bulk out for an ad for a health club. The girls look around at each other, because nobody wants to be the first to say like Buy me lots of expensive food, but after such a hard dance class and all, they could just about eat horses, so they all kind of nod together, like they could take it or leave it but taking it will be just fine.

Settled. The food here is atrocious, but would you ladies be interested in Chic? Sheena's med stud read their mind, but again they play it cool until Julie looks right at him and says, *Hot!*

The guys insist on paying for all the drinks, and of course they can't tell them they never pay anyway, and on the way out Yassir says, Good night, ladies, and you could tell the guys were impressed, because they probably just went in today for the first time, because they heard it was happening and that they serve cappuccino in old soda-fountain Coke glasses with a metal frame, like it was an egg cream in Brooklyn.

Out on the street, the bald guy, you know, Julie's, pulls out these car keys and heads straight for this pink Buick Electra convertible! They could just die, and the little runt is grinning like a shiteater, *pardonnez mon français*. If it were any other Caddy— except of course a stretch limo with a bar and VeeSeeAre like Sheena's dad's—it would've been Tacky City, but this one is like a real old boat and just droolingly gorgeous and *Vice*.

Well, they all pile in, and now of course Julie is like pressing her thigh into his and he is just about to burst his pants or swerve into the sidewalk he is so excited. Who knows why Julie has to do junk like that; she's absolutely gorgeous, with a way cute blond blunt cut, but she's probably banking on this guy having a king-sized waterbed he's so rich, because she says she comes like crazy on a king-sized waterbed no matter almost who's on top, even scuzzy François, the French You.Enn. ambassador's son.

They're in the Village now, and Julie's is hipper than they thought, because he knows his way around with no problem at all, and they pull up at Chic? and the doorman knows him already, and he trys to play it off like he hasn't got *beaucoup* bucks to stick a bill in the doorman's hand like he wasn't *really* trying to let them know he did it.

Chic? is a real swinging place, because it's real young but kind of expensive, so bums and stuff don't eat there. All the tables are this tacky Formica stuff, with plastic placemats that say junk like *Welcome to Garberville, California* or *Visit the Trees of Mystery. You'll be glad you did!* or *Everything's Bigger in Texas!* and below it's a picture of like a pig bigger than a truck or a cowboy hat bigger than a refrigerator. Around all the walls are all these racks of bowling balls, though there are no lanes, and hanging from the ceiling are all these TeeVee sets, but they must be tapes, because all they show are old TeeVee sitcoms and professional wrestling, no commercials. It's great.

Olivia says she's starved, she can't wait for din-din, and the other girls look at her, because they told her a zillion times never say *starved* in front of guys, but they were all starving anyway because of dance class and all, and if their body sprays wear off, soon they're all going to smell like horses and the guys are going to ditch them.

The waitress arrives, and the girls always crack up when they see them, because the waitresses all wear these old-teacher, rhinestone cat-glasses with cheap gold chains holding them around their neck, their hair's in curlers, and they have on these ultra-tacky, floral-pattern housecoats, you know, they look almost like raincoats, but lighter and buttoned from the neck to below the knees, and on their feet, real tacky fake-fur slippers, the kind your grandma wears if she's from the Midwest and born poor. The bartenders wear black shoes and straight-leg pants and dirty, tank top tee shirts under untucked bowling shirts that all say *Sal.*

Aw, what'll it be, you rich teen scum, says the waitress like always as she smacks her chewing gum and like leans on one hip like she's mad.

Richard the model and his friends order Texas Ranger Slab-slingers, which are really just double hamburgers and baked beans, but good, and cheap beers. And Dorothy orders an Oklahoma Onion-Bunion, which is a hamburger with corned-beef hash and onions, and a Margarita, and Julie and Olivia do the same, but Sheena has a Junior Slabslinger and a Margie, because she's afraid of getting bad breath, but if you drink the Margie after the burger you're fine.

Olivia's remembers the last time they were here, they got really trashed. And Sheena's med stud says, Yeah, he was so wasted he ate like six or seven orders of french fries. The guys all laugh about getting high, but the girls, especially Julie, are like all ears now, because if anybody's got cocaine Julie will jump their bones like that (snap).

The food arrives on these like frozen-food compartment trays, only they're not tinfoil but almost silver, which is a pretty decent idea, and the burgers are tasty but the fries are delicious, because they're real salty and greasy and come in big buckets with french-fry pictures on the outside like at a drive-in or someplace tacky, only the bucket looks like it's paper when it's really ceramic.

They hang there for a while, then all decide to hit Spazio, because Richard is friends with the bouncer so he should comp them all in. And Julie's says, Let's all do some lines in the car.

They pile back into the car and Julie's puts up the roof automatically, which takes a long time but is a gas, so they can all party without being paranoid or anything. He sets off for Spazio, which is close to Chic?, while Sheena's opens the glove compartment for the coke. The ride is *so* smooth, Sheena's can cut it right on a mirror in his lap while they're *moving*. They double-park in front of the club, and there's a big crowd of poseurs whining to get in, and Julie's whips out an already-rolled-up hundred, which is kinda tacky and *déclassé* but the girls had never done it before, so it was kind of a thrill, and they snort away (*ffff*

ffff ffff ffff) and Julie's got her hand on her guy's knee and he's smiling, and Richard's holding Dorothy's hand. Olivia and Sheena and theirs are a little cooler for now. Richard gets eight of them comped in, which is impressive at twenty bucks a head otherwise.

Spazio is hopping for a Monday, the music is hot, the police lights and strobes and sirens are just kicking like the whole place is electric everywhere and Dorothy and Richard go on the dance floor and spin and bop like maniacs and together they make a great couple because she's gorgeous of course and he's an absolute hunk and they're dancing real wild because they don't care who's looking, and even though they haven't known each other long they're into some heavy sexy pelvis action and Julie pulls hers out to dance too only he can't dance for anything but she's practically making him come in his pants the way she's all over his hips and just a minute later they go back to the car and you can guess what they're up to because coke makes her go crazy and the other girls are all flying too but with Yassir always on Olivia's case she doesn't need this guy just for the itch and Sheena's her usual ice-cool and Dorothy's got LeVon over at Carver but she's really going wild for Richard anyway with her hands all in his hair and his in hers, and if he's got his own apartment who knows what will go down, because who wants to take a train uptown that late alone she sure doesn't and now Richard's hands are on her hips and he's poking once in a while but he isn't as big as she'd have thought but then again it's not the meat it's the motion that makes your baby want to rock and not hurt too much but none of that on a first date so take it slow and keep them high and dry for a while no matter how much you want it, and yes it's not fair, but life isn't as they say and besides you didn't make the world you're just trying to make the best of it even though it's sometimes cruddy and all it's all we've got, right, so what can a girl do but hold on and buck with the waves, buck with waves? ride with the waves or buck with all four of these guys even Julie's has a great tush which is real rare but important because it tells a lot about performance which is more important than many women let on especially women their mothers' age they'd just lay there and let the guy split them in half and say nothing or even, Thank you I had a very lovely evening, but that's crazy what with Gee spots and all if they can ever find it just press and WHAM! Fireworks City and then it'll be fooling around like rabbits and Happy Days Are Here Again but for now it'll be controlcontrol-control no matter how much blow they plow into you ladies, even pot though pot's harder because it really gets the juices flowing and you could almost go down on animals it's so strong like your stomach's falling out of you and somebody turned on the heater and you just want to get COOL and grab someone on the dance floor right there and hump away just about to have the Big Ohh of your life of your whole life like knee-shaking feet up in the air and screaming and biting your hair just like in the flicks.

That was some really good shit, huh, says Richard.

Yeah, says Dorothy, it was Oh Kay. Then even Dorothy smiles at such a lie, as the other girls dance over to her, and they're all just smiling because that was the strongest they've ever had, ever, and they're laughing because Julie's already out in the car and it's only midnight.

Richard takes Dorothy upstairs to the lounge and they sit on a couch in front of the pile of sideways and upside-down TeeVees all showing the same EmmTeeVee of some blonde with big boobs looking at herself in a mirror, then smashing it, and a short-haired stud in sunglasses driving an old car. Richard puts his arm around her shoulder like he's done it a million times before, then leans over and kisses her. He's a good kisser, no banged teeth or anything, and she's a terrific kisser, at least she always says so—blacks almost always are, she says—but Sheena always objects, because she says you can't stereotype our race. Anyway, they're going at it now heavy-duty tongue action, but Dorothy won't let him feel her up right there in the club. If it were Danceteria or the Palladium for sure, because she doesn't know those people, but here no way, she hangs here all the time. Richard says he wants to go out to the car because he feels they really have something special, but Dorothy smiles and shakes her head. Then he says, How about your place, his condo is being renovated, which means his parents are home sleeping.

Some other time, she says, giving him a peck on the lips.

You mean you're leaving, it's just midnight, and she says that she's got to catch the train back uptown and pack, then catch the red-eye Amtrak to Springfield and school. She already missed today's classes, so wants to get back for tomorrow's afternoon Art History final. Dorothy's the best liar. They finally both decide to get together again when he comes back from a shoot in Florida in two weeks, and after he asks a couple times, she writes her right phone number for him. She kisses him again, this one long and lots of tongue, but only enough to get him chubby again, then goodbye. She goes downstairs and gives Sheena and Olivia cheek kisses, and outside Julie's guy's car is dark but she sees Julie's hand squish against the car window over and over again to his beat.

Girl, now take off your slippers, Cinderella night is over. I'm not psyched for this train ride shoving all my jewelry in my Le Sportsac and having to stick my chin out and look all ugly and mean but those damn cabs wouldn't go uptown for shit. Rich is great looking and has a hot body but he's dumb as wood, still if me and Julie double we can do it right there in that boat of a car. You've never done it in a

car before and it'll be like the movies. But it's funny how his Buick is so chic and whatnot because everybody knows he's a prep and not a pimp or Mister Jefferson, the Fayva Shoe King. Yeah, this class shit is crazy, but after college and biz school I won't have to worry about that no more 'cause it'll be Morgan Stanley investment banking and Fifty Grand a Year City, yeah buddy. No more crashing on Julie's or Olivia's floor like a slave 'cause you absolutely cannot train it past one. Yeah, I'll have me a dee-luxe apartment in de skyaaaay. I'll out-booj even Sheena only hip not just snooty, rich and black . . . I hope Mom'll let me off work tomorrow, what a drag. Still it's kinda cool after these wealthy preps start talking about their dad the TeeVee producer or world-famous microsurgeon, for them to say, What does your father do—or mother, don't think I'm sexist, and they laugh and you say, My mother runs a diner in Harlem and my father's in Texas somewhere. And just once I want some Graham or Brett or Ethan to say, You're joking, but they never do 'cause they think I'll rip their dick out. Look mean, look mean and this asshole crazy bum'll keep walking, there's a cop in the next car so don't sweat, good, go bother that off-duty pro. "Las cucarachas pueden entrar, pero no pueden salir." The cockroaches can get in, but they can't get out. It's cool learning Spanish from ads on the subway, but shit, I'm already bilingual though it's getting harder to talk to the pro downstairs. What was that word she laid on me the other day for blow-job? Drano? Say, Richard, want a Drano? Pardon me, Dorothy? Drano man, you want a Drano or not . . . Hey chill out, it's fo you, not for me. That would be too funny. Bobby would've cracked up. For a Jewish millionaire's kid he's pretty hip. I kinda wish he'd write but I guess YouEssSee must be Party City day and night. Los Angeles. What a life. Funny how the group was just swinging last year, everybody had their senior and their cherries popped, but this year's been mighty dry except of course LeVon and those gorgeous Princeton soccer players. We are some wild, dirty chicks sometimes, but all in all we are all right even though I'm sure Sheena thinks she's better than me but *that's her black booj hang-up not mine 'cause I'm no Black American Princess. . . . God I just hope Mom'll let me slide tomorrow. Poor is poor but I can't get psyched to get drooled on by winos all afternoon. That's pretty wack. And I just can't relate to being cooped up in that plastic cage like a slave. It's gonna kill me. I'd love to find a job near school at a Haägen Daz or one of those New Wave card shops or of course at a boutique. Still, I need beaucoup bucks to hang with my crowd. I can't wait to retire at forty-five and never have a boss and just sip tall drinks on the porch of my mansion in the Virgin Islands. Goodbye ghetto.*

30

Dorothy steps from the train at 125th and looks across the girders and tracks to the far token booth and her godfather inside. SWEET DREAMS, DARLING, he says into his microphone, but due to faulty wiring she hears BLEERT DORPSCHTICK. She blows him a kiss, then walks quickly—head ballerina-rigid—across nearly still Lenox Avenue to Fifth Avenue and her apartment building. During her first year at private school, when she was ten, she told the other students just that she lived on upper Fifth Avenue. Before unlocking her building's outer door, she makes sure the light inside is on. If it is dark in the hallway, she either waits to enter with another tenant or for a squad car to pass. She opens the elevator door, waits for its inner door to automatically scrape open, presses 3, and waits for the hum and the upward jerk. Unlocking her front door locks, she enters and relocks the door. The velour couch is still shrink-wrapped with thick, clear vinyl. The mantel over the plastic logs and red light-bulb fire still supports the graduation picture of her big sister. Shawniqua's head leans over a shoulder as if the Yale mortarboard were too heavy a weight. Next to the gilded frame a note from her mother tells her that Aunt Nadine is sick again so Darcelle will be nursing her all night. Dorothy presses the glass face of the new, black, remote-control television. It is still warm.

I know y'all's up, so don't even try to hide it.

In her brothers' room, she hears bodies sliding between sheets. She opens the twins' door to see Don and Vaughn lying in their beds, their eyelids closed so tightly they wrinkle. She kisses them both on the cheeks. The twins each rub at the spots.

Night, you cute little fakers, and in the morning remember to leave me some corn flakes.

She closes the door triumphantly (*clickk*). Giggles bubble from the joyous room.

In her own room she steps down from her red pumps and drives them into the closet with a kick. She unzips the bottom of her pegleg jeans, unbuckles the belt, and inhales to slip her thumbs inside the waistband to unbutton the top button, then pops out the other four buttons. By bending one leg, then the other leg, she rotates her bottom out of the pant seat. Then it's one last firm push over the thighs, and the jeans slouch dead to the floor.

The blouse she unbuttons before the mirror, turning to watch the light smear and shine over the silk over her breasts, the deep-brown mounds revealed slowly as her nipples extend hydraulically. She turns to see how her panties curve with her hip and how—by rising on point and flexing her bottom—each buttock becomes a ball. She fingers the light switch down (Off) with her free hand.

December 26, 1984

Dear Sir:

I must now confess that your writing challenges me. Though you persist in this suicidal and unforgivable penchant for pornography, I must admit that this latest passage on Dorothy is not altogether without merit. The dialectic between class struggle and cultural assimilation, the mental anguish of rising (???!) from a middle-class Harlem household to the rich, white, New York, controlled-substance-abusing elite is almost interestingly handled. Of course you then proceed to ruin it all with more misogynistic belches, where women control every eroto-romantic encounter—always to the detriment of the male. It is this naive, wrongheaded, and backward assessment of life that will continue to fetter your lofty literary aspirations.

As for the "joyous room" crack on page 108, this cynical swipe at my prose style (very successful and oft-awarded, I might remind you) was not as vicious as your having had me killed with that frying pan—truly a low point in this very rough draft. Are you finally beginning to heed my earnest and well-meant advice? It is gratifying to see, finally, the tempering of your excruciatingly nomadic prose style.

About *my* contribution to your novel. True, I began these consultations without an eye toward the publication of my own segments, yet I would be less that honest were I not to admit that my editor has expressed an interest in the piece. Of course you will be remunerated for the use of your characters' names, so fear not. My lawyer is drawing up the contract.

I also know the director of a black advertising firm there in New York. Perhaps your talents could be more lucratively exploited as a copywriter. I have already given her your address, so you should be hearing from Gloria at the start of the new year.

With the utmost sincerity,
Isshee Ayam

P.S. I truly wish you and yours a most merry Kwanzaa and a Happy New Year.

P.P.S. Your stand on negritude, sir, continues to befuddle me, and I would be interested, and perhaps the authorities would also be interested, in knowing if your apartment looks onto a certain Italian dance studio.

12/31/84

Dear Ms. Ayam,

I usually do not write personal letters while still on a book's first draft, but your letter of the twenty-sixth prompted this swift response.

You are absolutely correct. My prose and my thoughts have changed, tightened, and—if I may be so bold—improved. Is-shee—may I call you that—for after just having read and thoroughly enjoyed your *Chillun o' de Lawd*, *Hog Jowl Junction*, and *My Big Ol' Feets Gon' Stomp Dat Evil Down*, I feel a real intimacy between us; even though you can know only my latest piece. Unfortunately, my major work, *Hackneyed*, is still only available in manuscript form and, at that, only in precious few "serious" bookstores.

More on *Platitudes*. I feel I must explain myself, and forgive me if I am more confiding now than our past, adversarial relationship had allowed. Last year, after an ugly incident too complicated and sordid (and a story as old as those of noble Chaucer) to detail, my wife left me. Not only was I emotionally devastated, but she—as a well-connected matriarch of the black New York bourgeoisie—stranded me from all financially advantageous situations in this city. Needless to say, it has been a very lean year. Consequently, I am afraid the stress of my "real life," especially during this, my first holiday season alone, has invaded my narrative. An unforgivable occurrence professionally, I am sure, but nonetheless an all-too-human one. If I should again stumble, please understand.

I am sure you are aware that on February 20, 21, and 22 at the Wellesley Hotel here in New York, the annual BAA conference will take place. I have always shied away from black author anythings, because I find them both pompous and aggrandizing, and controlled by hacks and phonies like that Afro-Florentine expatriate sham Richard Johnson (who is Dorothy's male-model friend's namesake, by the way). However, if you are planning to attend, I would be delighted to meet you face to face.

Oh, and thank you for the job recommendation; however, I am afraid that for now at least I am committed to the full-time life-style of the starving artist. Yet if *Platitudes* never does find a kindly publishing house, I might very well be calling your friend.

In New York I can be reached at (212) 719–9800. If for any reason a recorded message tells you the number has been disconnected, do not be alarmed. I am currently having a rather trivial dispute with the phone company that I am confident of resolving shortly.

Your colleague and fan,
Dewayne

P.S. As for your publishing your version of *Platitudes*, please do not do anything rash. In my current state, I cannot protest too loudly, yet I am confident that we will be able to work something out.

P.P.S. I have often wondered why you never allow your picture on the inside cover of your books, so have been curious to associate a face with your stirring prose. A very short while ago I discovered your splendid interview in *Newsweek* magazine and was very pleasantly surprised to find color photographs of you at home and attending your aerobics/self-defense class. Not to be overly obsequious, but you have nothing to be embarrassed about. At all.

Still, to correct my unfair advantage, enclosed is a fairly recent photograph of the "real" me.

31

Earle had a dream Monday night. An important dream.

He's on the deck of an indoor pool somewhere, probably in Manhattan, only there are trees and bushes and a duck somehow, just like Lake Wanawanabe up at Camp Winamac, where Earle went for five summers. There are people in the pool, maybe it's crowded. He's wearing street clothes and shoes, and sees Dorothy in the pool. She swims to him, moors her elbows over the pool's edge, smiles at him. He lies flat on the poolside on his stomach, but doesn't get wet. He kisses her on the lips once and is not even scared. She looks right at him and smiles even more.

Smiling, Earle awakes Tuesday morning. It must be a sign, he says as he sits up, kicks the covers to the floor. Then he snaps his fingers and says, Right! He throws the rope of sheets back on the bed, he leans his head out his bedroom door and sees her door is open. At this hour she has almost always left for work.

Mom?

He slides his robe onto his arms, over his shoulders, holds it closed around himself, and looks into her room. Her bathroom door is also open.

Mom?

He looks into her bathroom and sees no one. In the living room, no one, and no one in the kitchen. He tears a trash bag from the roll (*brrrrrrrd*), jogs back to his room, closes the door, and lifts a corner of his mattress. Unzipping the leakage cover on the boxspring reveals, spread flat and colorful, his pornography collection: ten white women on the covers of heavy magazines, nine of their mouths straight, and their eyes very serious, long hair lifted by off-camera fans; the tenth, his favorite, looks surprised, her mouth a wet, red O and her eyes comically wide as she handles a microphone-thick candy cane. He sweeps all but her, December, into the tall kitchen trash bag. Over his bed he drops this magazine, staples down. For a beat it rests balanced and stiff, vertical, then it curls around in half—an Ionic column. December's one-piece swimsuit is now rolled down under her breasts, her fingers are in her hair, and her eyes radiate.

Goodbye, says Earle as he opens his robe.

After a quick click at the front door, Earle hears: Earle? You up yet? It's raining and I forgot my umbrella. He shoots December into the bag, yanks his robe belt too tightly around his waist.

Morning, baby, hurry up, it's a school day, remember. Oh, and tonight we're going out to dinner with Nat, so come home straightaway. Bye.

Another sign, he says. Again he looks out his door, watches the dining room, sees no one, but this time bolts the front door. Why on earth did you bolt the front door? he has his mother asking. But Mom, you always say you can never be too careful. [Grins.] Back in his room he carries the bag in his arms to the kitchen. Most likely he is afraid of any holes that would reveal the bag's contents, or even worse, any structural flaws along the seams that would let drop everything—a steam shovel/tyrannosaur opening its jaws.

He pulls the used kitchen trash bag out of the tall kitchen trash can (plastic) and drops his bag inside the other. The orange peels, milk cartons, cardboard fast-food hamburger cradles, ice-cream boxes, empty pesto jars, and still-dripping-clear-red-juice white

Styrofoam raw-meat trays camouflage the *Playboys* and *Penthouses*. Nevertheless, out in the hall in front of the service elevator, he puts the trash bag in front of his *neighbor*'s door.

32

In JayVee field hockey, Friends zero, Carver ten, announces Dr. Wyte from the speaker, muffled by the stack of felt erasers. First period will begin one half hour late at nine-thirty today because Misses McRae's Human Behavior class is conducting a schoolwide survey. She assures me that your answers will be completely anonymous and requests the utmost maturity in this matter. Your candid, honest results, she tells me, are the key to the success of this experiment.

Students, I trust you will heed our headmaster's precautions, adds Mister Morgan. I have read this survey and frankly admit that some rather intimate questions are being asked of you. However, I am confident you creatures will not try to look at each other's answers. Furthermore, anyone caught snickering, giggling, laughing, or even chortling will be hung by the neck until dead [students laugh] . . . Miss Rosebloom, please distribute the questionnaires to your classmates.

She cradles the stack in her left arm and efficiently distributes the dittos still smelling thickly of duplication fluid. When she arrives at Earle's desk, he stares at his books. But she waits and wobbles above him until finally he looks up. She is pale with hate. She turns away, unsteady, and slowly finishes her route.

FRIENDS SCHOOL SEXUALITY SURVEY

May 8, 19——
Ms. McRae/Hum. Beh.
Note: ALL answers will remain ABSOLUTELY anonymous. Your candor
and honesty and earnestness and maturity will help us a lot.

Please circle the correct responses.
1. CLASS: Sr/Jr/So/Fn
2. SEX: M/F
3. AGE: 19/18/17/16/15/14/other _____
4. How would you describe yourself?
   a. Studious   b. Athletic
   c. Artistic   d. Alternative
5. Have you ever had sexual intercourse? Y/N
6. If no, why?
   a. Not yet had the   b. Waiting for love
      opportunity
   c. Waiting for marriage   d. Do not want to
7. Have you ever performed oral sex? Y/N
8. If no, why not?
   a. It's perverse   b. Not yet had the chance
   c. Waiting for love   d. She (he) will not let me
9. Have you ever had it performed on you? Y/N
10. If no, why not?
    a. It's gross   b. Not yet had the chance
    c. Waiting for love   d. She (even he) thinks it's
                               gross
11. Have you ever masturbated? Y/N
12. How often? Note: Male average—1/mo.
                     Female average—1/2 mos.
    a. Once every day or more   b. Once a week even
    c. Once a month   d. Less than once a month
13. When you fantasize, do these things make a difference?
    (Circle as many as true.)
    a. Age b. Race c. Lingerie d. Technology e. Part sizes
14. Describe your first sexual experience (from kissing to going all
    the way).
    *On a roller coaster with this friend of the family, a girl in Georgia.
    I put my arm around her and could have done a whole lot more
    easy.*

15. If you have still not had any sex, then when do you think it's ever going to happen?

    Listen, every day I wake up and I hope it will happen, every single day I hope a girl in my class or a famous movie actress or somebody will stop in the street and say, "Wait, you're really cute, you know that? I don't care what everybody else says or that your skin is bad, I'm falling in love with you right before my very eyes at first sight." Sure it's rare and might not ever happen, but then again, who knows, right? If it does I'd be the

16. What type of contraceptive do you use?

    happiest kid in the world and my whole life would be perfect, so of course I hope it'll happen every day. What would you do wake up and say, No, I hope I'm depressed and crazy all day long and for the rest of my life? No, I want to be like

17. If you or your partner were to become pregnant what would you do?

    all those movies where the goofy but lovable guy sees this super-beautiful and sweet and everything sexpot and pesters her and does crazy romantic stuff for like most of the movie, and at first she thinks he's a jerk, then something happens and she finds out how really special he really is and they kiss for hours and

18. And if she did not want to have an abortion?

    hold on to each other's heads and make love, but it's not like porno or Playboy or nothing like that, because they really love each other, so it's okay and beautiful and I mean that.

19. Have you ever been in love? Y N

20. If yes, please describe.

    I'm going to describe anyway, as long as I'm here, because you guys should ask us people who have never been in love the questions, because we're the ones who need all the help, not all those football players and cheerleaders and models and artsy-fartsys who have been going out with people since sixth grade. They're normal, so why ask them anything. But listen, I met this girl uptown, way uptown, and just saw her for a minute, but I'd marry her and quit school and forget about

21. Did sex help or hurt the relationship?

    college and become a night watchman or a museum guard just to buy her things, that's how really romantic I am, because Love is all there is. Everybody says so, movies, songs, books, so who cares about Ph.D.s and good schools, and I'm almost a junior and we're supposed to care about this stuff a lot and I do, don't get me wrong, only if you gave me one wish it'd be this girl falls

in love with me, not a scholarship to Caltech, and for a soph-
omore, that's pretty deep if I say so myself because

22. Do you feel comfortable discussing sexuality with your parents
or guardians?
*I know many seniors who just think about school and couldn't
care less about romance, but they'll find out when they're rich
and half dead what they missed. See how I think? I think someone like me deserves to find love if I want it so bad, right? But
everybody says it'll break your heart, or life isn't fair, but if life
isn't fair, then what's the point, and if you get your heart broken,
that's an experience too and it's better than being like a computer just spitting out the same thing,*
Thank you for your cooperation. We hope to inform everybody
about our results next week.
every 1 × 10⁹ times like living on automatic pilot.

Every one of you little miscreants finished? Good. Rosebloom,
allow me to call upon your assistance again in collecting the ver-
idically completed questionnaires and delivering them to my desk,
thank you.

Janey pushes herself up, her fingers on the wood veneer, her
thumbs down the metal curve of the desk, her knuckles white—
wax.

Well, come on, child.

Janey releases the desk, deflates to the floor. Mr. Morgan
runs to her, and Earle, Andy, and Donald, the three closest
to her body, kneel around her. Janey looks up at the class, reels
up her cheeks, but her eyes are too wide and afraid to fake a
smile.

People, first-period classes are beginning and I have play rehearsal, move along, give the girl some air . . . You boys, I am
afraid I must ask a favor of you. Uh, since we are in dress rehearsal,
I-I cannot afford to miss today's practice. If you would be so kind
as to accompany Miss Rosebloom here to the infirmary, I will
explain to Commander Considine your tardiness. Thank you very
much.

I'm fine, Mister Morgan, I can make it there myself, she says, while standing slowly, her head heavy and low.

Nonsense, but I must be off . . . Boys, I'm trusting you not to exploit this liberty.

I really feel fine now, guys, but it's sweet of you to come with me.

It's nothing, Janey, says Earle. You can faint anytime it gets us out of class.

She looks at him and laughs, and pink begins refilling her cheeks. He laughs, too. At the nurse's station she says, Thanks, thanks a lot.

33

Shawn, their food server for this evening, has just told them their choice of salad dressings and is now holding a small chalkboard with today's specials.

Never mind them, I will have the New York Strip Sirloin, medium-well, Idaho baked potato with sour cream *and* chives, the double-sautéed zucchini, and I will try your house creamy garlic-and-herb on my salad, says Nat Mee, captain of the Twenty-third Police Precinct. His voice is deep—the mechanical growl of heavy machinery.

I'll have the Crabs à la Picaresque, the potato buttons with bacon and Monterey Jack cheese, the juicy home-fried broccoli sticks, and I think I'll also try your house dressing, oh, and another Kir, says Earle's mom.

May I please have the chopped sirloin, please . . .

Certainly. How would you like that cooked?

Medium, I guess, and the sweet-and-sour vegetable jumble,

the potato buttons with just bacon, and I'll have the French dressing, please.

Another iced tea?

Earle looks to Captain Mee.

Of course he will have another iced tea.

Nat, Earle's lost some weight since the last time you saw him, hasn't he? He goes running in the park every week.

Congratulations, son . . . Your face does seem slimmer.

Oh, and today, Earle, on *Live at Five* they asked Nat about being one of the few black precinct captains in the city.

It was not much, really. I just told them the essoess—same old stuff. Told them that we need more smart young black men and women, like yourself in a few years, to join the upper echelon of the force. But we also need ordinary black police officers. I said it seems absurd that we are the lion's share of this city's private security force and traffic-control officers, yet only a handful of its police force. And remember, we represent over twenty-five percent of the city's population.

I taped it, Earle, if you want to take a look later on. Oh, and I have the best news of all, Nat, how could I have forgotten. Earle, I'm quitting that damn, nasty, racist South African Airways and am going to be the spokesperson for the city's Health and Human Services Commission!

Wow, that's great, Mom.

Isn't it! And the AychAychEssSee is all run by black folks. The director, Myron Washington, knew your father at college. So no more bombs going off in airplanes to talk about, no more protests at the office. It was downright embarrassing walking past all those demonstrators every morning.

Your salads, says Shawn, their food server for this evening. He places Captain Mee's salad in front of Captain Mee, saying, House dressing. He places Earle's mother's salad in front of her, saying, House dressing. He places Earle's salad in front of Earle, saying, French . . . Fresh pepper? their food server for this evening adds as he displays his long wooden pepper mill.

Yes, please/ease, say Captain Mee and Earle's mother. No thank you, says Earle. Shawn carefully yet vigorously twists the top of the pepper mill over each of the adults' salads (*grrrrrchgrrrrch/ grrrrchgrrrrch*) and exits.

Maylene, I am truly excited for you and your new position. You have some fantastic opportunities for advancement. Remember, I have always told you that if you play your cards right, and if our mutual friend wins next November, you can almost count on being the press secretary for the new mayor himself. Captain Mee forks lettuce hearts, eats them.

Oh, don't you go putting ideas in my head now, Nat. I hate expecting something's going to happen, almost *knowing* it's going to happen, then what happens? It doesn't happen. I remember once as a little girl, it was near Christmas time and I knew my folks had hidden my little, useful presents around the house, but my big gift, the one I'd been whining and hoping for since the summer, was this brand-new red bicycle I'd seen in Mason's Hardware downtown. Anyway, a week before Christmas, like I said, I was with my sisters, we passed by Mason's and the bicycle was gone. I asked Mister Mason (a sweet old white man who let us folks into his store well before he had to), I asked him where'd the bicycle gone to and he just smiled like that old Cheshire cat and said somebody'd bought it. I was afraid for just a minute, then I thought I understood everything, and was skipping and singing all week long. Come Christmas morning and it was storming and hailing like the dickens, the shed door was banging *smacksmacksmack* and I remember thinking the whole thing was gonna blow away and smash something, it was so windy. My father put on his coat and boots over his pajamas to go out to that shed, and I was so excited, and I remember Mama telling him to be careful because those escaped convicts might still be out and about somewheres. Well, he went out to the shed and brought back—well, guess what he brought back—this mangy, old, *old* bicycle, not the pretty one I'd seen at Mason's at all. And you know what happened to my pretty bicycle? Shreena Corinthians, this girl everybody hated who lived just down the route, was getting *my* new bicycle for Christmas, but the escaped convicts stole it to make a getaway, but it was storming too bad and they were knocked over in a ditch and it was smashed. So I'm telling you not to expect anything until it happens.

Chopped sirloin? says their food server for this evening, Shawn, as he hinges open the food-serving stand and on it lands the big metal tray with the three plates and two drinks. He lands Earle's plate in front of Earle.

New York Strip Sirloin? . . . As the man with the food lowers the plate in front of Earle's mother, she leans back into her chair hard and quickly crosses her hands before her.

Oh! I'm so sorry, madam. You had the Crabs à la Picaresque. The first plate lands in Captain Mee's sector, and Earle's mother's plate rests before her with a Here you go and Sorry for the mix-up . . . Anything else? . . . Enjoy.

How's your hamburger, Earle; it looks good, asks his mother.
Fine, Mom. How's the crab?
Delicious. You two want some?
No thank you/No thanks.
Captain Mee pours a small button of steak sauce on his plate, asks Earle how would he like a job after school.
Earle looks up from his food, swallows too much meat, pushes the ketchup stain off the side of his mouth. What kind of job, sir? I study a lot after school.
Well, as you know, I am the sixteenth congressional district's Democratic supervisor and we are organizing a voter registration drive for this spring, because there is less than a month to the

Democratic primary. I am sure I need not tell you that Al Robinson, one of our own, is trying to oust Mayor Feld, so if we want him to have a fighting chance, we will need to register as many of his likely constituents as possible. You won't get paid, but it's for a good cause and it's an excellent opportunity for you to get to know Harlem.

Of course Earle'll only be working in the daytime? asks his mother.

Of course . . . Well, son?

When do I start?

I am proud of you. Tomorrow afternoon would be fine.

Oh, be careful, honey, but I'm sure you'll be all right. Use your common sense. Take the bus, not the subway.

Everything all right, folks? asks their food server.

Delicious, says Earle's mother. Captain Mee and Earle both hum their agreement.

Would you care for some dessert? We have Creamy Chocolate Torte Deluxe, that's a fresh-baked torte crust filled with creamed milk chocolate similar to a truffle filling, with finely chopped hazelnuts mixed in, all topped with fresh dairy whipped cream and Bulgarian bitter-chocolate shavings. Black Forest Cake, which you are already familiar with, but here it's a thick and creamy chocolate layered sponge cake topped with fresh dairy whipped cream, Bulgarian bitter-chocolate shavings, and a non-artificially colored maraschino cherry. French-Fried Ice Cream, a scoop of homemade Vermont ice cream wrapped in a delicate French pastry batter similar to a crêpe batter, then quick-fried in fresh peanut oil, keeping the ice cream frozen yet the outside crispy. Our ice-cream flavors for today are Kahlua, a Mexican, coffee-based liqueur; Amaretto, the famous Italian almond liqueur; Cappuccino, made with imported espresso beans fresh-ground daily; stoned-wheat thins for the calorie-conscious; Mango chutney; Cassis, the French black currant liqueur; Baci, made with real imported

Perugina hazelnut-and-chocolate candies; Nutella, a creamy chocolate-and-hazelnut paste by Rochet, and Strawberry, made with only hand-picked New Jersey big button strawberries boiled down over pecan wood flown in daily from La Fourche Parish, Louisiana. We have strawberry and chocolate mousse, again made with all fresh ingredients; New Hampshire apple, Monterey Jack cheese, Vermont blueberry, strawberry, double-French rhubarb fresh-baked pies either *à la* or *sans mode*. Mississippi Mud Pie, which we do a little differently than some restaurants because our crust is made of graham-cracker crumbs *and* Bulgarian bitter-chocolate shavings and small porcini mushroom caps. Cheesecake made with only Pennsylvania fresh cream cheese, again over our special crust, with either apple, blueberry, or rhubarb toppings. Macédoine, an all-exotic-fruit salad, and Jello-O.

Coffee for me, says Earle's mother.

Coffee here also, says the captain. But Earle here, what will you have? You must have something.

How is the Mississippi Mud Pie? Earle asks.

Fine, responds the food-serving Shawn.

34

Captain Mee has just driven Maylene and Earle home in his old gray Cutlass. Since it is warm tonight, Earle waits for his mother on the sidewalk. In the car he sees them squeeze hands goodbye.

Mom, you could have kissed him goodbye, I wouldn't have cared.

That's none of your business, Nosey Rosey, but anyway, I wouldn't feel comfortable in front of my baby . . . But what about you? Do you have a little friend?

I don't know.

What do you mean, you don't know? You can tell me, honey. I'd like to know.

Maybe.

Ohhhh! [smiles] Baby, that's terrific. What's her name?

Dorothy.

Is she a friend from school?

Uh, yeah, sort of. It's kind of complicated.

Well, anyway, honey, I can't wait to meet your little friend. I bet she's pretty. Is she black? I hate to ask but . . .

Yes.

Why didn't you tell me before? I'm so happy. Your father would be happy, too. Lord knows he was no lady-killer either, good-looking but very shy. I practically had to ask him out on our first date. I'm sure you've heard it a thousand times, but he took me to Le Vieux Chapeau, this swanky restaurant in Georgetown, and at the end of the meal he reached into his jacket and— he'd forgotten his wallet! Luckily, that day I'd been paid at the diner I was working at after school. He was so embarrassed.

When do you start your new job, Mom?

Next Monday, but I've got to straighten things up at EssAyAy this week. Oh, and that reminds me, I'll need you to go to the grocery store tomorrow after school, I mean after work, and bring home some empty boxes. It's going to be a bear, just a bear moving out all my stuff. Still, it'll be great to start working for black folks instead of against them, but then again, the bills had to be paid.

35

*Better hit the hay soon because I'm really going to see her tomorrow
and I don't want bags under my eyes. I'd just die if she said yeah,
the little roly-poly runt is kind of cute only he's got hound-dog eyes,
like somebody hung weights down off your eyelids or you're dead or
something. She must live around there somewhere, maybe on top if
it's her mom's place. I'll just stroll on into old Chez Darcelle and act
like I'm surprised to see her and say something funny like I won't
bump into you this time, and laugh and maybe touch her arm, no you
maniac don't go pawing her right away but maybe I'll say, Remember
me, I'm the guy who ran into you Sunday/crashed into you Sunday,
I hope you're all right, and then she'll squint and frown and finally
remember me and then the ball's back in my court and what'll I do?
Maybe say something like, What time do you get off work, but I can't
say that because everybody says that to waitresses. You just have to
begin saying, What time do . . . and they already get it and think
you're a jerk, but I want to know so what am I going to say? When
does Darcelle's close, I'll ask her, and she'll say blahblahblah and
I'll say, Wow you work late, that's a drag, and then what? Maybe,
Are you a registered voter? I could come around when you get off work
and register you/yeah, that's right. I work up here in Harlem too, you
know Nat Mee, the police captain and head of the blahblah Demo-
crats? I'm his assistant so if you need anything just holler/Oh by the
way, if you need anything just holler. Why yes of course I've heard
of the Cotton Club, yes let's go there and listen to jazz music and
drink cocktails or if you want, I know a great little place on the Upper
West Side called Picaresque. Then I could go there before and give
that Arab guy at the door ten bucks to pretend he knows me so I can
say "The usual" and she'd just flip. How's about you and me doing
it up in style? What would you say to a candlelight dinner for two at
Windows on the World? Don't think I say that to many of my women*

but you are absolutely the very most beautiful, you are, and I mean that from the bottom of/the depths of my heart/I really mean it, honest . . . Some guys just hand girls lines like they were fishing for trout, but I am sincere. You are going to go out with me tonight, I say right into her eyes. What, you've got another date? Break it . . . So I'll see you eightish. Super./Here's my money miss for the bill . . . Why yes, there is a little note on the back of my check . . . You are even more beautiful when you blush. Let's make it eightish, shall we?/Whoa there little lady, you've got a habit of crashing into me, not that I'm complaining you understand. I kinda like it. How's about you and me blowing this clambake and getting ourselves a little grub?/You know that old corny line about love at first sight? Well I didn't believe it until just a moment ago, when I first set my eyes on you./Raise your head a little more, to the right, there! Perfect, yes, you'd make the perfect lead in my new big Broadway extravaganza . . . Oh I'm not really a big-time Broadway producer, or even an actor or anything. I'm just plain old me, but all those things I said about how dynamite you were are still one hundred percent true. I just knew that a hot potato like you would never go for a guy like me . . . What? You knew all along? But you like me anyway? Hurray!/My father isn't really the billionaire owner of Johnson Products, the makers of Ultrasheen, Afrosheen, and Ultrasheen cosmetics . . . You like me anyway? You knew all the time? Yippie!/I'm not really the star of The Boy Who Tapped His Way Out of Trouble, *just everyone says I look like him . . . You knew from the very beginning but liked me from the start? Yeah!/You know when I said I was the blockbuster best-selling author of all those teen spy books, well, I . . . What? You knew from the word go? Ya-hoo!/Yo, why's a foxy mama like you hangin' in a place like this?*

36

Boys and girls! Boys and girls! Please help me in this operation and be quiet, please. Commander Considine is serious. Now I have an important meeting with a representative from the Digital Corporation about our new AychDee fifty-one high-speed printer, so will not be able to complete our lesson today, but please, I am trusting you all. I expect you to complete the assignment on the board and leave your signed printouts on my desk. Thank you and see you all tomorrow.

Earle, Andy, and Donald had all three already finished the homework while he was talking, only Donald finished a second earlier than Earle and Andy for once and would have mailed

HA HA

to each of their screens, only after that text-editor thing, of course Considine found out, so built some new protection into the system. Now Andy and Donald are playing Dungeons and Dragons, because Andy's father bought him a subscription to ComputerWorld and he pirated the program from there, even though it overloads his memory. Earle's trying to debug this Civil Defense program that's supposed to tell everyone where's the nearest empty bed in a bomb shelter in the city. He's doing it just for fun, but also to kiss Commander See's ass after the you-know-what episode. Earle now hears this loud huffing from in front of Andy and sees Janey breathing loud, like snorting through her nose, and holding her hair. She's no airhead at all, because she just won a prize for a poem she wrote, but when it comes to computers she's a real spaz. So Earle leans into his VeeDeeTee and asks her what seems to be the trouble.

I just can't get the hang of this FOR/NEXT loop or even the IF/

THEN thing for that matter, she says, so Earle gets up and asks her what it is she doesn't get, and she says everything. As he's leaning over her looking at her screen and explaining what's supposed to happen, her perfume goes into his nose and it smells like sunshine, and her sundress exposes the whole top part of her breasts, which inflate and deflate as she breathes. Sure he notices it all right, but he's no two-timer . . .

You mean the IF screens the possibilities and only lets through the ones it wants and the THEN takes the possibilities and does something to them? she says.

Andy looks over his terminal at Earle and winks, then makes a ring with his left hand's thumb and index finger, and pokes the hole in and out with his right hand's index finger, all right behind Janey's head. Donald's behind Andy and is just cracking up.

Listen, she says. I'm having a party this Friday night at my house and you and Andy and Donald are invited. It's at ten o'clock, ten-forty Fifth Avenue, apartment seventeen bee. You guys were real sweet yesterday to walk me to the nurse's.

Earle's never even been talked to nice by a pretty girl before, so he blushes and his brown skin kind of glows red underneath. He goes back to his station and switches off his terminal at the exact time the bell rings, like his switching off the computer switched on the school bell.

37

Earle is now out of school, away from his friends, on his way to work in the train. Knowing Earle, he is probably nervous, but hopefully less nervous than he would have been at the beginning of this book.

At 116th he pulls his day pack from between his legs, slides himself to the gray plastic train bench's edge. At 125th he is the first to the street; yet, having forgotten to draw a map, he has forgotten north. A man in a red, black, and green crocheted skull cap and a long white robe suggests that Earle buy some incense, but Earle declines, asks the man which way is the Jean Toomer Democratic Club. The man says that it's over that way, brother, and points. His white robe sleeve loops low from his arm—a yawning mouth.

The right half of the club's stoop has just been painted. At the top of the stairs an old man proudly looks at the reflecting, wet green. He walks down the unpainted side of the stoop, stopping to touch up the fifth, sixth, and ninth steps.

Bet you wouldn't have thought of this, Earle, says the old man, handing Earle the paint can by its metal loop, the brush by its sticky handle.

How do you know my name?

Never you mind that, he says over his shoulder as he resteps up the stairs. Earle begins to follow, but is stopped by the man's pointed finger. The old man paints the air with his left hand.

Coat number two, youngin.

When Earle finishes, he enters the building and is talked to:

So, if you're finished with that, put the paint over there by the door and get yesef by me so I don't have to holler at you.

I'm sorry, sir, I did not catch your name.

That's 'cause I did not throw it at you, boy, says Stevie, grabbing a baseball from a warped and unstable shelf. He pushes the ball quickly at Earle's face. Earle jerks out of the ball's flight. It bounces on the floor, into the storefront window, and makes fall three large cardboard posters of Al Robinson, Your Next Mayor.

If it'd broken, guess who'd've paid for that window, and it wouldn't be Stevie, that's for sure.

Stevie?

What? This old geezer is too old to be a Stevie, you say? Well, I was born a Stevie and I'll die a Stevie, and you get to work.

Earle is not happy. He asks, Why are you so crotchety?

Well, how else do you expect a thin old wisp of an old man caretaker to be?

Well, good afternoon, Earle, says the old man. Captain Mee told me you'd be coming round. I'd shake your hand, but I wouldn't want to get paint all over them nice school clothes . . . How do you like the stoop? See, I had to paint only one half at a time, elsewise you couldn't come in or out till it were dry . . . Oh, forgive my manners, but you know how us old folks get. Stevie's the name, Stephen Freeman, but folks round here have been calling me Stevie from Jump Street, so I guess that's what you can call me too . . . What? I'm a bit hard of hearing, you know us seniors, so you'll have to speak a bit louder than normal, but you won't have to yell. I'm not deaf, not yet anyway, praise the Lord . . . You hungry? We got some doughnuts over here donated by the ladies in the doughnut shop across the street, and coffee, tea, and that instant cocoa stuff. Help yourself.

No thank you, sir. I just had lunch at school. But could I ask you a question?

Shoot, son.

Who is this Al Robinson Captain Mee was telling me about last night?

That's a good question, son, because he's the whole reason we're here. He's a black man who wants to be mayor of the city of New York. The primary between him and Mayor Wesley Feld is on June twentieth, then, of course, the winner of that goes up against whoever them Republicans can find in November. Thing is, we have to register all our folks before June third which is in less than two weeks now, because that's the deadline for voting in the primary. And that's the whole kit and kaboodle. That's all you need to know . . . I've got some straightening up to do in here before the rest of the recruits show up. You just make yourself comfortable.

The Jean Toomer Democratic Club's door holds a poster of Al Robinson, kindly serious. The wooden floor is old, yet clean and flat. From the proud walls stare collages of familiar faces: Malcolm X, Frederick Douglass, Sojourner Truth, Harriet Tubman, Martin Luther King, Jr., Stokely Carmichael, Amiri Baraka, Angela Davis, Huey Newton, Bobby Seale, John Carlos, Marcus Garvey, Sekou Touré, Jomo Kenyatta, Patrice Lumumba, Albert Luthuli, Nelson Mandela, Paul Robeson, Jean Toomer, Jesse Jackson, James Baldwin, Ralph Ellison, Richard Johnson, LeRoi Jones, Richard Wright, Toni Morrison, Alice Walker, Stevie Wonder, the Jacksons, and every major jazz artist ever.

On the bookshelf in the back stands a small library of worn Afro-American paperbacks. Earle sights down his finger at one title, another, another, until his finger arrives at a thick brown book. He hooks his finger over the top of the book and, by pulling downward, rotates it out and free from the shelves' strong compression. A woman of color, her nostrils flare, a shredded straw hat on her head, in her mouth a long dried-grass stalk, her eyes burn from the cover of the book. Over her head the words *Hog Jowl Junction* and *By Isshee Ayam* and *Best-selling Author of Heben and Chillun o' de Lawd.* Under the artwork: *The Uhuru Contemporary Afro-American Fiction Series* and *Soon to Be a Major Motion Picture!* On the book's back cover: *"Ms. Ayam's prose . . . burns with the glow of righteousness, sparkles with the fire of a richly endowed imagination, and shimmers with the light of a brilliant and creative technique"—The New York Review of Books.* And below that: *Jewelle Wilcox, a sharp-witted, fiery young black girl feels trapped in the small Southern town that doesn't understand her insatiable drive for fame, knowledge, and perfection. But when Slyde Slim, the good-looking, smooth-talking zootsuiter, arrives on Main Street in his shiny red Hudson, Jewelle believes her prayers have been answered.* [new paragraph] *In this beautifully depicted Mississippi summer of 1938, this young girl, so naïve, yet so gentle, learns some very important lessons about life, love, and loss. Her tears and her laughter, her all-too-familiar groaning, growing pains of sexual awakening, are here exquisitely rendered as naked truth to anyone who has ever been blindly in love.* Lower still: "*A gem of a novel . . . a rare treat . . . a triumph . . . If you read one book this year . . . one of those books you devour, not read, and after having turned the last page are left dazzled, awed, stunned—and hungry for her next masterpiece*"*—Richard Johnson, The New York Times Book Review.* Inside, on the book's last page Earle reads: *Isshee Ayam was born in Tallulah, Georgia, in 1948 and studied English literature at Spelman College, Atlanta. After beginning English graduate studies at Yale University, she suddenly decided to devote herself to writing novels—instead of critiquing them. Her first work,* Good Lord, Gimme A Good Man!, *was published in 1973 and won her the coveted Saltonstall Fellowship at Mount Holyoke University. She recently received the Rockefeller Book Award for* My Big Ol' Feets Gon' Stomp Dat Evil Down. Turning to the back cover, on the very bottom: *Cover design by Eva May Jones/Fiction/ISBN: 5-085-9866-7/US $4.95/Can $5.20/GB 2£50p*

Stevie, sir, can I take this one home? Earle holds the book toward the man.

Sure you can, take as many as you want; that there's a sort of lending library. You take a book, bring it back, maybe bring an old one of your own. Stevie now moves his eyes from Earle to the front door. Earle turns around to see five people, four black ladies and a white young man, walk up the dry side of the stairs.

Hello, volunteers, how y'all doing this fine day?

Fine/ine/go/ood/good.

You all already know which corners to take, and the pens and registration cards are over there by the bumper stickers. I'm going to show Earle here—he's our newest recruit—how to fill out the cards, what to say, and the likes.

Stevie does just that. Trust me.

Earle has been assigned the northeast corner of 125th and Lenox. If he were to fall backward, his head would bruise on the doormat of Chez Darcelle.

Operation Dorothy, all systems are go, he whispers.

Many Harlemites pass him and glance at the book of registration cards he cuddles.

Excuse me, ma'am. I was wondering if you were registered to vote, by any chance? When Earle started the question he was talking at the side of her face; when he had finished, he was looking at the back of her blouse collar. Four paces after passing Earle, she stops, looks slowly left, then right, but continues this head turn to behind her, now turning her shoulders, hips, and finally her feet. She looks at Earle's eyes and pokes her chin at him. He steps backward, holds the pile of cards to his shoulder so the words REGISTER TO VOTE! can speak loudly.

The woman squints and nears. Oh! she says. I thought you was one of them odd religious folk, and I don't need but one Lord in my life, praise Jesus.

Are you registered to vote yet, madam? The deadline for voting in the all-important Democratic primary is fast approaching.

Why no, no, I'm not. Should I be, son?

If you are not registered, you cannot vote, and if you would like a say in who wins the primary, Al Robinson or Mayor Feld, you must be registered before June third.

Well, you *know* I like Robinson. He's one of us and a good man.

Earle gives her the card and the clipboard and the pen, points to the boxes to X, the spaces to fill, drops all the other cards, picks them up, and realigns them poorly.

Thank you, son, you make me proud.

Are you registered to vote? . . . Are you registered to vote? . . . Are you registered to vote? . . .

Excuse me? says someone female.

Turning, his eyelids burst wide and his chest convulses.

Dorothy, she says, pointing at herself. We ran each other over on Sunday.

I'm—

Earle, yeah, I never forget a face. My mom saw you getting into your voter-registration action, which is cool 'cause it's for the cause and all, and she told me to bring you this soda.

That was quite nice of you. I truly mean that, uh, thank you.

Earle, you're sweet. As Dorothy was saying *sweet*, she touched his forearm. She is now walking into the diner.

I want to crouch way down low go oooooooh! and jump and twist and shout YIPPIE! *but I won't but I could because I'm gonna be happy forever and ever and ever.*

Earle holds his cheeks in his hands and squeezes the hot blush from his face.

Hiya, Earle. Day two of your registration action, huh. But as for me, I'm just so happy it's Thursday—EssAychEyeTee. Get it? I see you're still hanging on this corner, but it looks kinda slow, so I guess you're just mellowing here *wid de old fo'ks* that don't work.

Yes, I have only registered six people so far, but many say they have already registered.

What with Al Robinson and all, a lot of us are getting into it and voting for a change. But all my downtown friends are still going to vote for Feld.

Oh, are you from the Upper West Side, Dorothy?

Naw, but I guess I am pretty tame for a Harlemite, *n'est-ce pas?* I go to St. Rita's and they kinda ruined me.

I attend Friends Academy and live on Ninetieth Street and Riverside Drive.

Oh, I hang near you at Picaresque a lot.

Oh yes, I go there frequently. *You talk like a fuckin' robot in front of her you goombah. I wouldn't be surprised if she bursts out laughing or spits at you.*

She looks inside his eyes. Well, here's your root beer. She squeezes his arm. See you tomorrow.

God if she looked at me for just a second more I'd've spontaneously combusted and left just a smoking pile of clothes.

Earle, it's here! TeeGeeEyeEff. Between work and school, come Friday I'm just wasted. So just get me into some *human* clothes so I can freak out all weekend long.

Yeah, I know what you mean. I am real tired—wasted—my-self.

So what are you doing tonight?

I'm going to a party, I guess.

Great! Me too. I swear if I don't let loose soon it's Funny Farm City, you dig? . . . Oh, my mom says if you want something else than root beer, just holler. Don't be shy.

39

When she asked me what I was doing tonight I almost pissed 'cause I thought she was gonna ask me out. But when should I make my move is the big question. She likes me and all but I don't want to come on like some gigolo who just wants to bone her 'cause I couldn't care less about that stuff and for me that's really saying a lot and I could just sit there and look at her smile for days like a dopey goon and I wouldn't even care what people say 'cause I could just like climb into her eyes and live there forever. But maybe I could say, Hey what about a movie? And she'd know I like her and she could say yes or no, or maybe I'll just be honest and say, Hey I like you a lot and would you go out with me, but no no you goon, that's too heavy, she'll think you're trying to marry her or something, which actually would be pretty fantastic and our babies would be skinny and great-looking and smart. Still, this time she didn't touch me goodbye, I wonder what she's trying to say?

40

Well, have fun at your little party, son, but be sure and be home before one. Here's cab fare. You look cute [smackk].

Earle, Donald, and Andy meet at the corner of the Metropolitan Museum of Art and Fifth Avenue, because Andy swears all the best-looking girls in the city pass by there. Trinary synchronized watches in Commander Considine's class, so they are all here at the corner at twenty-one hours and forty-five minutes on the dot and their three electronic watches all go off together *chirp-chirp/chirpchirp/chirpchirp.*

So is he gonna tell them where he's been after school or what, Andy asks Earle, but Earle just says he's got a job, but Donald says that Earle's mom says that he only goes to work till five, but he's never home before dinner, and then finally Andy says straight out that Earle, he's changed. So then Earle just shrugs his shoulders and they all look at their watches, and since Janey's place is on Eighty-sixth and Fifth and they're now on Eighty-first and Fifth and it takes one minute to walk a block and a little bit in an elevator, they start walking now because it's twenty-one fifty three.

As they're walking, they talk about Camp Hav-a-Byte and how it's going to be great and how much they're going to learn about programming and get away from the city, and it'll be great college suck on the old transcript. Then Donald asks Earle doesn't he think it's weird, Janey inviting them to the party after what happened with their text editor and all. He means, because everybody thinks they're goons. Earle says he thinks it's because they helped her when she was sick and Andy wonders if she's dying.

This humongous stretch Lincoln cruises up in front of Janey's building. It's all black and has those three Lincoln Continental fish gills on the front fenders like a shark and a black TeeVee antenna on the trunk that looks like a modern statue. The smoked rear window goes *hmmmmmmm* and this great-looking black girl looks out at the awning. The driver goes and opens the door for her, and behind her come two terrific-looking girls, a blonde in a black-leather miniskirt and a brunette in a red one. All three are wearing these bright-colored high-heeled shoes that are Trinary's favorites. They all go inside the building, and by the time the guys are inside too, the doorman is hanging up the intercom and saying, You can go up now, girls. Andy yells, Hold that lift, please, and Donald and Earle could just die, because when Andy says *lift*, that means he's going to go into his phony English accent and wreck everything. The girls say they're going to a party like they want to hurry up and don't think the guys are invited, but Andy says them too, and says Janey Rosebloom's party, they're Andy Williams and friends, and the doorman, a nice guy, calls up, gets it straight, and then lets them up.

At Janey's floor the girls pile out and book, and then all stop quick, giggle real loudly, then go inside to the party. Earle tells Donald that if Andy says *lift* one more time, he's going to punch his lights out, and Donald just shakes his head like he can't believe Andy acts so stupid sometimes.

Dingdong goes the door, and as it opens the music zaps them and Janey sticks her head out from behind the door and really smiles when she sees who it is. The guys go inside, and she takes their coats and says to make themselves comfortable. Those three girls are on the couch, their naked legs like right there, and Janey says the bar's over here and points to a real bar, like in a bar bar, and there's all kinds of booze. Andy says he's gonna fix himself a screwdriver, probably because it's the only drink he knows, and Donald says, Me too.

Earle, let me show you around the apartment, says Janey as she walks with him through the living room to the dining room. The den, she says, opening a door to a large-screen TV, five-foot-tall stereo, and a pool table with a Tiffany lamp staring at the table's green felt center. She opens the next door just after having said, My father's bedroom. The room vibrates brown: wood and smoked glass and tortoiseshell. . . . My room she says, pushing open the last door of the corridor to a pink room, pink walls the background for James Dean, Modigliani, Matisse's *Blue Woman*, and an old Richard Gere poster. In the room's center extends a pink canopy bed—a healthy tongue saying Ahh. Earle says it's beautiful.

Oh, it's gross, I know, but I haven't changed it since I was a little girl.

The two re-enter the party, and after Janey has said how glad she is they've come, that they've all been at the school now for ages yet don't really know each other at all, she cries, Bill! at an almost bald guy she runs to and hugs in the living room. She'd like Earle to meet her boyfriend, Bill.

Way to go, Ace, Andy whispers to Earle. She's already got a squeeze, and Donald's right behind him, saying that Earle's been faced royally by a guy who's practically bald, but Earle says that he likes her just as a friend now, but of course Donald and Andy are like Right, sure he does. Donald tells him to be more realistic. Take those two girls over there, for example. One's a zitface and the other's a tub, so they'd be perfect for them.

Just now somebody important must be at the door, because those terrific-looking girls get up from the couch and scream to the door, except that short-haired blond one who's holding hands with some guy. Trinary tries to pretend they're not looking like a bunch of geeks, but they are anyways, and in comes this knock-out black chick looking real cool.

Hot, Dorothy says to Janey. Her apartment is real hot, and they peck each other on the cheek, smiling like they are best friends, which is OhKay because they used to be real good friends last summer at cheerleading camp; even Sheena, Olivia, and Julie like her. Anyway, Janey's no BeeOhOhSee—bitch out of control—even though she goes to Friends, and those girls there are like megawild. So right after they all like hug and say hello at the door, they go off to the corner, where Olivia says to Dorothy to guess who's here and the heavy-duty boyfriend of Janey, and Dorothy says Who? and Olivia says Mister Pink Buick Electra convertible, that's who, and his name is Bill, Julie didn't even know his name, and Julie comes over and calls Olivia a bitch, she just forgot his name, and he is just bad news anyway, no matter how hot his car is. Dorothy laughs and asks Julie what she's going to do now, but Julie says What does she mean, what is she going to do about it, nothing, because see that hot-looking *uomo* in the

Armani jacket. He's hers and *he's* worth a cat fight. And she goes back over to him and Armani puts his arm around her waist.

Dorothy's just got to look over there at those three nerds, those two black guys and the white guy, or maybe one of the black guy's mixed, anyway, the white one yells, *Hold that lift* when they were downstairs, like he was English or something, and they had to wait there for hours for Janey to figure out why they were crashing her party. Then Dorothy is like, Earle! but nobody knows what's she talking about. The doorbell rings and Dorothy says that must be LeVon, he found a parking space quick.

Andy's been nodding his head, pretending to believe Earle when you know that he really doesn't, so he says that sure he knows her, sure he knows her—in his dreams. His wet dreams. Then Andy shakes his hand over his crotch like he's whacking off, but Earle goes, Andy's a pig sometimes, does he know that? And Donald says, Well, if she is from Harlem, why's she dress like *that* . . . Now *he's* from Harlem. The guys are looking at this humongous black dude who looks like he could rip out the door and Donald swears he's that All-State tackle for Carver named LeVon, but everybody calls him Mongo, and then he puts his arm around the pretty black girl that Earle says he knows and she puts her arm around him and Andy says, Strike three, slugger, and Earle walks away real quick.

Earle walks stiffly toward the bathroom—a windup toy soldier. He hits the door. Julie and Armani are in the shower stall. The shower-stall door is open. They are about to begin the sex act, it seems. Earle urinates, spits into the toilet bowl, exits.

In the corridor he stands, his back a bit away from the wall, his arms shoelaced over his chest tightly. He hinges from his ankles, leans back, his shoulders hit the wall (*thud*). He does not move his feet under his shifted center of gravity. He does not unlace his arms. He pushes his shoulders off the wall, twists back to standing. He falls back again (*thud*). Repeat.

I can't believe it. She's not only got a boyfriend but he's Gigantor the Thunder Tyrant. I should've known. She's too beautiful for you fatso, why can't you just settle for a tubby acnehead with halitosis who hates you.

Oh, there you are. Didn't you see me? When you said you were going to a party I didn't know it was this one! I forgot you went to Friends with Janey, but when I saw you with your buddies I said, Girl, that looks like my honcho Earle . . . I'll be right back. I've got to use the bathroom.

It's occupied, he says as a moan seeps through the door.

Oh my God, that's where she went. Dorothy slides her hand, her arm, under his elbow to hook his arm. They walk to the living room and sit on the couch.

Her thigh is right against mine, it is, but there's enough room for her to scoot over if I made her sick or something but where's that big moose, just my luck get killed by a monster and not even do *anything.*

You know, Earle, I been thinking how funny it is how we're both commuters, sort of. Of course it's different since you *live* down here with them. But still, like here we two bridge . . .

Le's dance, says Mongo, holding his open palm down to Dorothy.

One second, LeVon, I'd like you to meet Earle. Earle, LeVon . . . Oh, and, Earle, I'm not working Monday so stop by, I live real near the restaurant—Twenty thirty-two Fifth, right across from your Democratic Club, apartment three Gee . . . OhKay, LeVon, lead the way.

And of course Donald and Andy say, Jesus Christ, how does he know her? She's a knockout, not as great as Janey maybe, but a regular babe, and nice of her to talk to him instead of that giant who Andy thought was going to cream Earle at any minute, he was so mad. Next time believe him when he says something is all Earle says about it, acting real cool. Then Donald tells Earle about those two normal girls and how they gave him and Andy their numbers, so he's going over there to ask her to dance this slow song. Donald goes over there and Andy says him too and starts walking, only like a motorcycle-gang leader or something.

LeVon's all over Dorothy, he's so insecure and immature, like he has to compete with a fatso nerd when he is like this giant wall of muscle, not too smart, but sometimes a girl's got her mind on the other thing. So now he's grinding all over her, almost poking a hole in her dress, it looks like; yeah, he's acting like Sheena's tomcat that used to rub that stink tomcats have all over everything in the house to show it's his until they got him fixed. Then Julie comes back from the bathroom smiling, and Olivia says she can't believe her, she's going to catch a disease. Then over at the front door that chubby black guy Earle that Dorothy says she knows and his creepy friends are taking off, so as they're saying goodbye to Janey (who's looked better), Dorothy waves over at Earle and says, Stop by, she means that. Mongo like turns her around and jabs her with it, but this time you can't really blame him.

41

Why, Earle, I thought I told you not to show up here when it's raining, says Stevie. Rainy Mondays are the worst. Ain't nobody going to want to stop and fill out no soggy piece of paper. And I was hoping to finally get to that other half of the stoop too. Want a doughnut?

Thank you, sir.

Now what's this sir business, don't make me keep telling you to call me Stevie . . . Well, as long as you here, let me put you to work. You can start by helping me move these tables out of the way so I can mop the floor. I want to make this place spic-and-span, because tonight Captain Mee's coming in to do the *real* politicking.

Stevie, is Al Robinson really going to make a difference?

The smile on Stevie's face falls to a flat, serious line. He raises a finger to Earle's cheek. Follow me, son.

Silently, Earle walks behind Stevie, through the hall to the rear window. Behind the Democratic Club lies a lot. There, browned metal tendons sprout from cement pillars crumbling. Below these steel-and-stone nests, a mud swamp holds waves rippled both by the fat, slow drops of drizzle and by the shiny black backs of swimming rats.

That lot down there, says Stevie, was supposed to be a lower-middle-income housing project called The Basie. You see, right before the last election, that Feld character promised if he was elected, the first thing he'd do is build this here project. Well, we black folks believed him and went out and elected him, and sure enough, his first day in office he had this big old parade up here and cut the ribbon and shoveled up a piece of dirt with his gold-painted shovel, and bulldozers and cranes came, and pretty soon those cement columns started going up. Then a month later Mayor Feld said the city was having money problems so *temporarily* stopped construction. That was six years ago. That man is no friend of the black man or the Puerto Rican man neither, if the truth be known. Ask Captain Mee if you don't believe it. He's a fighter too, and I for one hope he himself runs for something someday.

They walk to the front of the store as the hard-rock rhythm of the rain slows to a soul beat. Earle and Stevie squat a bit at each end of the long metal tables, place their fingers under the tables' edges, and stand and move sideways, their feet apart, together, apart. They move the other tables too, then nest the orange, plastic-seated, metal-legged chairs into each other in a column so high it curves. Outside, the rain noise stops, and again rise the sounds of sirens, cars, people, the dripping building's crackle.

Now get going, Earle. I want you fresh tomorrow, and we'll register the whole darn district.

42

Crap, my plans are always screwed up you can never count on nothing. It was raining so hard before, who'd've thought it would stop just like that [snap] If it were the summer you could say someone pushed you in front of one of those open fire hydrants with the child safety sprinkler cap but now what are you going to do . . . OhKay, OhKay, don't panic. You've got a whole half an hour before launch time . . . I've got it! A car! A car! Just say you were walking down the street when a car splashed you. What could be simpler. Yeah, just say that, and then you've got it made in the shade as they used to say, because then she'll ask you to take off your pants but remember remember remember it's not sexy it's just the way it always happens so don't get excited and pop a boner or you'll ruin everything. She'll give you her robe to wear while your pants dry and say you've got cute knees, you'll talk and she'll find out how interesting you are, then everything'll be quiet for a second, then you'll kiss.

43

Earle slides his hand into his front pockct, pulls out his wallet, un-Velcros the flap, slides out the tiny address book, and rechecks Dorothy's address. On 126th are five large water-filled potholes and the gutters are still flowing fast.

Earle turns his head left, right, then turns around. Since more than half the brownstones are empty—sheet metal blinding the windows and gagging the doors—no one else is near. In the gutters, strange small things float, and oil slicks shine in four of the puddles. Earle whistles as he walks slowly. Before the fifth puddle, he again scans, then inhales fully, falls down to do a push-up over the pothole.

HOOOOOOOOONNNNNNGGGG!

The wide grille of a car stops just above his head. Earle rolls to the curb, into the gutter's stream, jumps to his feet.

Tú, pendejo, estás loco, verdad?

Earle's school jacket elbows and forearms are gray from the wet. His pants drip brown water on his shoes.

Ready, he says with a smile.

2032 Fifth Avenue is not an ugly building. There is no doorman, of course, but the door itself is newly painted and the plastic covers on the names beside each buzzer, like the paint on the walls, are neither cracked nor yellowed. Earle looks at the button, 3G, and the name Lamont, raises his right hand; his right index finger extends, pushes the wall next to the buzzer.

Don't be a coward. Change your life.

He pushes the buzzer.

Yes, says a voice, over a loud, electronic hum.

Earle. It's Earle Tyner, the guy—

MMMMmmmmmeeeezzz

Inside, he pulls open the elevator door, enters, pushes 3. On

145

the third floor Earle follows the alphabet clues from 3A to 3D at the hall's end, then back along the hall's other side to 3G. He steps up and down in place in his still-wet shoes and pokes the doorbell.

Earle! I'm glad you could make it. Come on in. It's pretty tame here alone, I've just been mellowing to James and Bill— James Ingram and Bill DePopulaire.

Earle pulls his wet shirt off his chest—a sideways tent. He shivers.

Gosh! What happened? Get out of those wet things.

She grabs his hand, pulls him to the bathroom. She leaves him there, he strips, she knocks, asking for his wet clothes.

There's no dryer here upstairs but I'll put your clothes in the oven under warm. She returns to the bathroom door and holds her robe up to the door's crack for Earle to take. In the kitchen, water is boiling in a pan. Dorothy returns, now finding him in the living room.

Don't look at the fake fireplace, whatever you do. It's *so* tacky.

Earle sits on the couch, his knees together. From the speakers in Dorothy's room a saxophone complains sweetly. She hands him tea in a cup on a saucer. He pinches the saucer's far edge and sits with it on the plastic-wrapped velour couch.

A gypsy cab splashed me for no reason at all.

The tea will warm you up . . . You look cute in a girl's robe [laughs].

She sits next to him, so close her impact seesaws him up from the couch; his tea spills to the saucer. He pulls her robe's hem from the top to the bottom of each of his knees, pulls tight the belt; the robe's hem again rises.

Be careful your thighs don't touch these *très* tacky slipcovers for more than a minute, she says, or you'll be fused to them forever, especially in the summer. It hurts like hell.

Thanks. *Can't you say something you goon. Think clever think clever think clever.*

You don't talk much, do you, Earle?

Not when there's one as beautiful as you in view. I guess not. I don't know.

You seem more like a thinker type of guy, and that's cool. Where do you want to go to college?

EmEyeTee or Caltech.

Yuck! You don't think it might be a little boring at one of those technical schools? I mean, there're like practically no girls or social life at all . . .

I am so close I'm really going to kiss you but no! Down! You'll wreck it and scare her. Down! I'll just count to ten and do it, or maybe wait until her mouth is half open like saying pool *or* spoon *or something, she's so beautiful, perfect.*

. . . Do you ever feel weird in your clique? I know we're not supposed to say this after civil rights and all, but do you ever feel different just because you're black?

Talk about mules, food *or say* cool *again or I'm gonna die.* Yeah, I guess so.

You know, like there's the people you hang with over there and then there's you over here.

Yeah, I know exactly what you're saying. It's lonely sometimes. *Boo, coo, zoo, do, chew.*

I knew you'd understand! She squeezes his kneecap. He flinches. Oh, what did I do? she asks.

Dooo? But no no nononono no No NO! *You flinched, you jumped back when* she *tried to kiss you. Oh God, she hates you and thinks you're a homo.*

MMMMmmmmmooozzz

Hello? she says into the intercom. LeVon? Come on up.

Earle, silent, squeezes the couch's cushion suddenly as he watches the room—the bathroom door, the bedroom doors, the curtains. He runs to the oven, swings down the door, pulls out his warm, wet pants by a belt loop.

Hi, LeVon [*smack*], come on in.

Earle's holding the pants over the robe, over his waist. He looks up at Mongo. Earle raises both cheeks together but is still not smiling. Mongo looks at Earle's head, Earle's pants, Dorothy's face. Mongo's cheeks also rise, also smileless. He turns, leaves.

What's the mat—she asks after him. Then, Oh!, she says, he thought you . . . She points to his pants. What a duh he is. I hate the jealous type, but I'd better go explain things to the big baby. Sorry about this. Now, as she is talking, she pulls out from the oven Earle's jacket, socks, shirt, walks them quickly to the bathroom, lays them on the closed toilet seat. I'm sorry I'm making you book and all, but I've got to cut that crazy jock loose, and it's now or never.

When Earle exits the bathroom, Dorothy smooths his jacket collar by sliding her fingers under the warm lapels. Downstairs, on the street, she squeezes his arm.

See you tomorrow, she says. Root beer'll be ready.

January 20, 1985

Dewayne,

I use this familiar salutation because, after reading your last letter, I feel nothing but shame over my past conduct. I was catty and cruel because I believed you to be yet another misogynistic, insensitive cretin with a penchant for child molesting. I had no idea you were merely another heartbroken human being. Because of my new disposition to your work, I have decided not to have my story published—or at least not before negotiating with you a mutually advantageous settlement.

I believe *Platitudes* is now coming along rather well. The two-completely-different-types-fall-in-love Love Story is a time-honored favorite. If it was good enough for Shakespeare . . .

Your work is now also much less "sexy," shall we say. I am referring to page 140, where Earle enters the bathroom where Julie and Armani (wonderful naming!) "are about to begin the sex act, it seems." Gone are your extended examinations of a young girl's cleavage, or the explicitly inventoried nocturnal onanistic hobbies of our dear Earle. I am pleased.

I am also obviously pleased with your mentioning my books in the midst of your narrative. I reserve judgment as to the efficacy (and the sincerity???) of this passage, but I am embarrassed to admit having experienced a blush of pride rereading those very old reviews. As you know, I have never been a fan of you experimentalists, *per se,* and often find that school a bit too sure of itself and arch, yet I must admit that I sometimes envy your stylistic liberty.

However, this letter is not solely to inform you of my change of heart but also to let you know that I *will* be attending the BeeAyAy conference. Consequently I will be in New York City from February 21 to 24. I must admit I am very much looking forward to finally meeting you. As one of your more vernacular-speaking characters might report, "And then she's like, Let's have dinner or something."

Yours very truly,
Isshee

P.S. At City Lights Bookstore here in San Francisco I discovered your *Hackneyed* manuscript and must say I am coming to appreciate your tremendous talent. Though admittedly bawdy, it is also a very funny work. Also, upon reading your own "Notes on the Author" I was pleasantly surprised to learn that you left Stanford to become a field coordinator for SNCC in Maybeline. As you must know, Maybeline is just a half hour's drive from Tallulah, my home, in Lowndes County. I was also surprised to learn you were stationed in Benin with the Peace Corps. A colleague and myself visited Togo and Liberia in 1977. Now that I now know how to "read" your statements on race and race relations, I feel infinitely more at ease.

P.P.S. Thank you for your photograph. Oddly, I expected an overweight man (a grown-up Earle), or perhaps a great globular bush of a natural, long sideburns and a Nkrumah Jacket, as you wear in the old photo attached to your *Hackneyed* ms. I was quite surprised to see an athlete. Along with aerobics and dance, I myself enjoy swimming to keep fit.

44

One ticket for me and one for my date, says Earle to the movie-ticket taker inside her Plexiglas booth. She's over there—he flexes his chin at Dorothy.

How much do I owe you? she asks.

It's on the house, kid. *Keep it up, slick. Doing great.*

Each standing on a stainless-steel serrated escalator step, Earle asks her to watch this, he used to do this as a kid, and rolls a penny down the stainless-steel slide next to the moving black rubber handrail. The penny scratches quickly down the chute, flies between two moviegoers, to the small fountain below dedicated to the eradication of stammering and other chronic speech defects in our lifetime (*ploop*).

On the screen, a close-up of a DO NOT ENTER sign as one piano key is heard pressed and pressed again, many times, a lot. With Dorothy's left red pump toe, she pins the heel of her right shoe and lifts free her right foot. Now with the toe of her stockinged right foot, she holds the heel of her left shoe to pry free her left foot. She crosses her right knee over her left knee, her right foot and calf now dangle—a pretty pump handle.

Earle smiles and slides his right arm onto the edge of the armrest. Dorothy puts her left arm there too. Her right great toe, the dangling-pump-handle one that crosses to her left side, periodically touches Earle's right pants leg. His pants leg touches his calf. He turns up his right palm, the one attached to his right arm on the common armrest but she does not yet hold his hand, but she always can if she wants to.

Oh! We forgot popcorn, whispers Dorothy, restraightening her legs, stepping back into her shoes, pressing past him to the aisle and up. Earle lays his right arm on the top of Dorothy's chair. *An old tennis injury, gotta keep it extended/it fell asleep/just stretching out the old arm-a-rooni.*

Now a STOP sign stares from the screen accompanied by a lonely oboe note. Earle watches the light filling the porthole in the door at the top of the theater hill. The porthole darkens, Earle turns back to the movie, adjusts his forearm so the meatier, more cushioned underside caps her seat. Finally, she steps past him, looks at his arm on her chair back, looks at his eyes. Earle retreats his arm swiftly to between and under his thighs. He watches the white dash in the road turn continuous, then double up with another dash, then twin continuous lines. The music is now an electronic watch's *chirpchirp/chirpchirp*.

Want some? she asks. The SuperJumbo Tub o' Popcorn targets her lap, so Earle is careful to scratch up only a few of the topmost kernels.

Later she says, Sorry, Earle, but I've got to crash. I didn't get any sleep last night. I was at Spazio with my girlfriends. It's not that I don't like your movie, you understand. Dorothy crosses her arms. Lays her head on his shoulder.

45

Oh my God keep your shoulder stiff, If she feels the bone there she'll lean the other way. I can't believe it, I can't fuckin' believe it. What a smart move taking her to this stupid movie. She thinks you're so smart. Andy was right, some girls do go in for the brainy stuff. She's got the softest head I've ever felt in my whole life and her hair smells terrific, like love. Like love, what a cornbone you are but don't laugh! You'll jiggle her, let her sleep so she'll want to do something later, won't be too tired. God I can't believe it even though she looked at me funny with my arm on the chair, you should've left it there longer make her say, Hey move it will ya creep, put the ball in her court, always keep the ball in her court. Hope she doesn't feel my heart beating but it feels like it's going to break my ribs and pop right out of my chest and go hopping away up the aisle it's so worked up. I bet you can get a lot of exercise just putting yourself through all this junk with a girl. I bet I could kiss her good night if I really wanted to, not that I don't want to but no need to rush it and that way she'll know you're not one of those football goons that break hearts and let girls get pregnant then laugh when they ask to go halvsies on the abortion, no I'll show her that I'm sensitive which I am but not so shy anymore which is good because it was something ridiculous before but I'm changing now, she's changing me, I can feel it 'cause a month ago I couldn't've said, Dorothy you know there's this hot movie playing at Lincoln Center would you like to go? and she didn't even say, With who? like you thought she would and you hardly even practiced or anything, weren't even super-nervous, of course a little, but I did it and she said girlfriends *and the disco on purpose and she dumped her big jock for me and this is all just too good to be true.*

46

In the days to come Dorothy and Earle's friendship fastens.

Sunset on Fifth Avenue, buildings smolder orange, windows burn softly, hot pretzels and roasting foreign meats punctuate every corner. At Rockefeller Center, beneath that gold-leaf colossus that soars over all skaters everywhere, he kneels before her, delicately tightening her pretty white skates. Around they go, she, ice-dancing, touching her toes or lifting back a leg, never exerting, floating, while he, knees warily bent, hands spastic flailings, steps to the bronze rail, and pulls himself along. She, smiling impishly, circles behind him and pushes him, faster and faster—faster still—around the rink; he leans into her, joyful terror claims his face. His legs cross, down the couple goes, a shock, then exchanged glances, then lovely, bubbly giggles and an ice flake on her nose dissolving. *She now pirouettes slowly for him,* nude, soft toes comb the soft department-store carpet. The burgundy dress on her deep chocolate skin. Back into the dressing room, then quickly returning, the turquoise dress shimmers in the store's bright lights. Then, a soft yellow knit dress curves closely over the small of her smooth back. She smiles big, buys the yellow, laughs, again spins, leans on a hip. She lays her old pants and blouse in the dress box. Down the escalator, they both walk backward, trying to stay in the same place until they each step on the toes of a descending security officer, who curses the two as they bunny-hop down and away into the afternoon light. Behind the store's frosted glass doors, the guard's angry, waving fist dissipating. *Cars, distant sirens, buses howling like jets, trains rumbling low and domestic squabbling. Sounds intrude from all directions, yet he and she walk content.* Shiny streetlights glow yellow, hum softly, coat West End Avenue in tender light, yet the wind this night is strong and the spring raindrops fat. Trash cans on every corner hold back-broken umbrellas now reduced to wintered steel shrubs. Yet one *she finds* still has half its cape. She withdraws it, opens it for him, he holds it ahead. His arm naturally curls her to him under the quarter-dome of shelter. Then she swats the umbrella from his hand and jumps in a curbside puddle that splashes him, wets his legs and ankles. He chases her through the now dense shower, she springs into the bus's opening door and waves through the receding blue glass, blows a kiss to him through the wall of rain, blurring. . . *He stands on the street corner, cars pass but not many people.* He looks up the street and down it, even whistles a bit. A very old man nears and he readies the clipboard, its metal clip hot from the midday sun. When the very old man has voter-registered and struggled himself away, he sees her approaching, that smile of hers, impossibly even sweeter. She extends the soda cup to him, he reaches, she snatches it back and takes a long drag from the straw in his drink and opens her big eyes wide over the root beer's plastic lid. He pouts a silent movie actor's pout. She hands him the drink, then shows him the piece of cake on a napkin she has smuggled behind her back. He bites the tip, hands it back to her, she bites a piece, hands it back, he bites, she, he, until there remains but a chip of frosting. She bites it in half, hands him the evanescent flake. He somehow halves it too, leaving a crumb in his palm. Holding his hand warmly, she lowers her head to it, lowers her tongue to the spot. The wet warmth in his palm's eye radiating. *She steps so slowly.* In his living room, for him she dances, twirls, holds a heel, extends. Now she bends at the waist, her legs unnaturally, artistically straight. While she is folded, she presses her nose to below her knees. He claps: the sound echoes from the room, rippling . . . *Smiles pass from him to her and back.* The knishes, hot dogs, pink cotton candy, corn on the cob all smell richly. He buys a Nathan's low-cal hot dog while she rides the merry-go-round, the only non-child aboard. Leaning forward on the horse as the ring dispenser approaches, leaning back as it passes, she plucks ten rings on every lap, quickly discarding the mere metal ones. Finally she picks the brass and tosses it toward him as he opens to bite. The ring, by luck, rings the end of the dog. Tears wax in his eyes, happily blurring . . . *All is gray*, Central Park's springtime night fog smears the distant towers; even treetops are kindly out of focus. The carriage driver introduces them to Clara, the mare, and hands them a heavy plaid blanket. In the stillness, the driver soon sleeps as Clara marches through the fog. She's been down this path before (*clopop, clopop, clopop*).

47

Hi, honey, I'm glad you're home. What did you do today? . . . Oh, before I forget, Andy and Donald both called again, something about a model rocketeers' convention at Madison Square Garden . . . What time do you have?

Ten-oh-seven Ma.

Good. Nat's coming by to pick me up any minute. He says that that man who runs that Democratic thing uptown says you're a good worker. I knew you'd do well. And you know something else, Handsome Harry, I think you've lost more weight. Yes, I do! You look healthier, thinner, and I bet I know why.

Why, Mother?

It's your little Dorothy, isn't it? My baby's almost grown . . . But tell me, how old is she? Where does she go to school?

St. Rita's, Ma, OhKay? She's my age.

Wonderful! You know, when I was growing up, Catholic schools were the only ones that would let us in. Is she smart?

I dunno. I guess so.

Don't be shy, baby. I tell you about my boyfriends.

So then are you going to be home *real* late tonight? he asks, with his eyebrows raised high on his forehead.

Son, you may be almost grown, but you're never too old for a whippin' . . . Anyway, I think it's just wonderful. You simply have to bring her over sometime.

MMMMMmmmmmoozzz

That must be Nat. Tell Jerry or whoever's on duty downstairs to tell him I'll be right down.

She runs to her room, returns with her purse in her armpit.

How do I look?

Great, Mom, only your lips are a little crooked.

I'll fix them in the elevator. Thanks, sugar . . . Oh! Mister Wellington finally wrote. I stuck the letter on the refrigerator.

48

Monday. Finally she arrives. She has talked Darcelle into turning his usual soda into a jumbo chocolate shake. He thanks her, thanks her a lot.

Dorothy, I've got a present for you too.

A what?

The envelope is the same soft yellow as Dorothy's new knit dress under her orange rayon waitress jumper. Its flap is unglued, just bent inside the envelope's body. She digs a fingertip under the paper tongue, pulls it free. She pinches the sheet of folded paper, slides it loose and out. She unhinges the thick card. The words face her:

> A cradle, a star of small, dry, green
> leaves in which, overlapping, gently
> furred, unpointed red petals nest fat,
> cupped, stuffed, and centering a yet
> denser, soft, red petal knot. Mutual
> shadowing lays unorganized but complete
> gradations: thick red to black. On a
> petal tip sits a tiny water ball and
> from there stretches one very long
> star of light.

Thank you, she says. It's weird but sweet. She leans toward him from the waist, listing her head to the right, kisses his lips, leans back, realigning her head.

Got to get my black behind back in there behind that cash register like I got some good sense. See you tomorrow, kid.

February 26, 1985

Dear Dewayne,

More kudos. I really feel you are coming into your own now. These last passages are handled wonderfully and, above all, sensitively. The subtly beautiful way the relationship matured from mere sexual infatuation on Earle's part into a deep and lasting friendship thrilled me. It is rare to find a man who truly understands how splendid intersexual friendships can be.

Your semiotics movie was fun. I'm glad to see you can laugh at your own.

The scene with Mongo was nicely handled.

The springtime ice skating (?) sweet.

The "rose by any other name" is truly lyric. Congratulations.

Finally, Dewayne, of course I am tremendously sorry for mising you at the Black Author Association Convention. After our extensive correspondence, it seems a shame that we could not meet. When we had decided on possibly getting together during the conference, I had no idea Richard Johnson would fly in from

Florence, and since we had not seen each other for ages . . . The next time he is in the United States, I will make sure you two get to know each other. I realize you do not much care for his writing now, but believe me, Richard is one of the brightest, most interesting and of course gifted men I know—present reader of course also included in that list.

The invitation to visit San Francisco is always open.

Your friend
and colleague,
Isshee

P.S. I hope you weren't waiting too long. I tried calling the hotel's bar but it didn't seem to have a listed number. Sorry.

49

Yessir, June third finally snuck up on us, and darnit, Earle, if you didn't register more than all the rest of my volunteers put together. But today is going to be a big one—all them folks that was puttin' it off to the last minute and such. Just tell them it is now or never if they want Al Robinson, a black man, to sit in Gracie Mansion. That should put a candle under their behinds.

50

I brought you a shake and a grilled cheese, says Darcelle, because you been working awful hard out here and because today's your last day, isn't it? I'm real excited this time, 'cause one of us is finally in the running. You know, I've always voted Democrat, but if it's just another white man toting promises I won't bend over backward for him, no sir. But sure I know a certain gal who'll miss your company.

Where is she?

Oh, I thought she told you. She says she sick, but I think it's just a unscheduled vacation. You know how that girl is . . . Say, if you want to, when you get a break go on over with some hot soup, I'd appreciate it. But that girl better be laying up in bed, 'cause if she ain't she'll feel it from my hand. Here's the key.

THE CUB DETECTIVE SERIES PRESENTS
The Case of the Flexible Dancer

CHAPTER 49

She meets him, leaves her old boyfriend, stops seeing her girlfriends, sees only him. They ice-skate, go to Coney Island, ride through moonlit Central Park, she touches him often. He gives her a rose. She kisses him right on the lips. *Question:* Does she like him as more than just a friend?

Answer: Earle unlocks the building's front door, enters, then pushes it relocked. He walks up the stairs slowly, careful not to spill the special liquid explosive nitro he will use to blow open the door and liberate his love. Stepping along the third-floor hallway, avoiding the older planks more likely to complain, Earle smiles large, unlocks, leans into the door, strides long inside.

TA-dum! he proclaims.

Richard, the model, opens his eyes, closes his mouth, looks into Earle. In front of and below Richard the model's exposed white waist, a restless brown buttock hinges a brown body, down to grab its own ankles, nose pressed below its knees, all under an umbrella of soft yellow knit—A quarterback and his center.

TA-dum! TA-dum! TA-dum! Just a little more and I'll TA-dum too! she cries beneath her rhythmic and inverted dress. Only gradually does she understand the silence.

51

Yeah I just turned around and closed the door (I think I closed the door), walked down the stairs one at a time, walked outside, walked down the stairs to the subway one stair at a time, asked for three tokens because you can never have too many, the train comes, et cetera, et cetera. Nobody even gave me a second glance, nobody gave me two shakes or whatever, and the train was totally normal even though I had heavy lava inside me. Wow who'll believe me? Who'll I tell? Like a movie, only I didn't come back and shoot them in cold blood and make the small red flower of death bloom on their foreheads as the bullets from my trusty silencer enter their skulls but I don't even want to. No I handled it well, just turned around and left, only I can't remember what happened to that soup but I thought I'd go crazy on the spot or cry or something. When my dad died I cried, I think. Everybody else was crying, but this is a cartoon and a humongous black anvil marked TWO TONS *falls on my head but just bounces off and everybody thinks I'm all right for a second, then a small crack begins at my head and turns into millions of cracks that zip all over my body, then nothing. Then whoosh! I crumble to the floor just a heap of puzzle pieces . . . It was fun while it lasted I could say or maybe better luck next time, or there are other fish in the sea, don't cry over spilled milk, a stitch in time (whatever that means), better to have loved and lost, all's well that . . . and every day there are songs on the radio about how she left me for some other man so I guess every day millions of guys feel just like I do now, though that's a hard one to swallow . . . Now what do I do? Watch a little TeeVee when I get home? It's weird how no one knows how you feel on the street. I say Hello Misses Needham and Hello Jorge or Jerry and they don't stop me and say What's wrong, maybe you should talk to Dr. Sheldon. But if you weren't crazy before you sure will be now only maybe it's a blessing in disguise because maybe you're so weird you'll be famous maybe. And when* ComputerWorld *asks me how I did it, how I became the president of EyeBeeEmm, I'll just say, Well my dad killed himself sucking on his exhaust pipe until his eyeballs turned blue and then I caught the only love of my life getting fucked up the ass like a pig [laughs].*

52

Three socks lay on the floor next to the *ComputerWorld* cover hiding the *Hustler*. Earle picks up one sock, the other two stick to it, and he ritualistically smells their crusty parts before pushing all three through his other dirty clothes to the bottom of his hamper. He limps a little. After his shower, Earle spoons Cream of Wheat into his mouth in the kitchenette.

Earle, says his mother. Up so early? That's good, because an awful lot has happened. Let me see . . . You won't believe this but that Health and Human Services Commission job fell through. Budget problems and all. You know how this city runs. Or doesn't run, if you catch my drift. They were prepared to offer me just twenty-eight thousand, and believe me, in this city that's not even cab fare . . .

I asked EssAyAy for my old job back. Boy was I embarrassed, but they love me there so even gave me a raise. Can you beat that? . . .

Oh, guess who's in town . . . Solomon Levitt, my cute little millionaire friend. Tonight he invited me to Windows on the World and then he got orchestra seats to *Tap Fever*. After all I've put him through, he's still got a sweet spot for me, bless his little heart . . .

Camp Hav-a-Byte called to confirm your place on the bus Saturday. It will pick you up at six-fifteen Saturday morning on the corner of Broadway and Eighty-sixth. Your clothes should be ready tomorrow morning. I had Mister Wu put on the name tags. I know you think you're too old for . . .

Oh, and Doctor Sheldon's office called again to check up on you. I said that if my boy needs the doctor he'll call himself. He's almost grown, I said. So if you want to go, that's fine, son. With my new raise . . .

Bye.

It's still too early to leave for school, so Earle turns on the radio.

. . . in See sharp, by the Vienna Sturbenfeld Orchestra, Hans Anderlicht conducting. Now I would like to take this time to remind all the friends and listeners of Public Radio's Double-You Bee Oh Bee that pledge week is once again upon us. So if you would like to hear more classical music, twenty-four hours a day, plus the award-winning news program National Public Radio's *All Things Considered,* all without the gauchery of commercial interruption . . . *shhhhhhxtchkpshhhhhh* . . . Yea-h! Nothing like Beelzebub's, Death to All Teachers, Principals, and Lunchroom Attendants to get you in the mood for this Wednesday, the last Wednesday of the school year! Yeah! Only two days to go before FREEDOM, yeah! But don't be late now if you are going in today, but if you're playing hooky keep it where you got it for the hardest rocking hard rock and . . . *shhhhhhxtcphxtcshhhhhhhhxtcphtox-hhhhh* . . . and finally, the Duke's Creole Love Call. Right now get ready for *The Doctor Is In,* Doctor Seymour Sheldon, radio psychiatrist . . .

Good morning, listeners, and today, since I want to hear from each and every one of you suffering under the oppressive weight of emotional illnesses or crises, or even if you just need to talk to someone, we'll get started right away . . . Caller number one, you're on the air . . . On the air caller number one . . . ?

Hello? . . . Hello?

Yes, you're on the air, madam, and please be as brief as emotionally possible, we've got a lot of patients to get to. However, if you would like to visit me privately, my office is located at four twenty-one West End Avenue, and the number is seven two four, two zero one zero, that's seven two four, two zero one zero. Continue please, madam . . .

Yes, Doctor, my name is—

No names, please!

Oh, all right, well, anyway, as I was telling you, I'm a very attractive woman in my mid-thirties, so I have *no* problem whatsoever luring eligible bachelors . . . Anyway, I've got this thing for famous guys. Yeah, I know it's weird, but I can't help it.

Go on, yes.

So as I was saying, if the guy's a nobody, even if he has a great body and all, I might lead him on for a bit, hoping he wins the lottery or goes on a talk show or something, but when he doesn't produce, I dump him like a ton of bricks. But you see, if the guy's famous, I get all hot all over and videotape it (I've got quite a collection in my TeeVee room). Why just last Monday I waited around backstage at the Stevie Wonder concert, then did it in the Sherry Netherlands Hotel.

So you made love with Stevie Wonder?

Raheem. He's Stevie's bodyguard. Said Stevie was right next door the whole time.

I see. And how would you like me to help you?

Help? I'm fine. Just thought you'd like to know. [*clickclick*]

Caller number two, you're on the air.

I am a thirty-seven-year-old and work in construction. My problem is I'm too romantic. I expect too much out of people, out of relationships, out of life. I pin my hopes on pipe dreams, then am crushed when they dissolve into thin air. I am cynical now; one might go so far as labeling me bitter and hateful. But I don't want to be.

I see. I see.

For example, in the late sixties I was very political. One of the first Yippies. I marched on Washington countless times and was even this close to being arrested with the rest of the Chicago Seven. At the time, I thought we were going to "change the world/ rearrange the world" as Crosby, Stills, Nash & Young said. Then I found out one of the directors of my group was taking bribes to keep us quiet and disorganized. I am divorced and just recently thought I'd found someone special—and this is after all those dating services and humiliating personals ads and Catskill weekends. So of course I make reservations at Windows on the World and get tickets to a show, then of course she stands me up.

And how did that make you feel?

[*clickclick*]

You're on the air, caller number three.

Hello, Doctor Sheldon, I was going to go to your office but I'd be late for school.

I see. Go on.

I finally found a girl, then she two-timed me and so I dumped her. Mom said your office just called, so I thought I should tell you. But I'm going off to computer camp on Saturday, then I'll be helping my computer teacher at school for a bit.

Well, I could try and squeeze you in Thursday afternoon, but if not, you can always have your old slot on Fridays when you get back, Earle—I mean—oops.

[*clickclick*] *shhhhhxtccpcshhhhhtcpkshhhh*[*click*]

53

After school, Earle steps out of the main door onto the sidewalk. The rest of Trinary, Andy and Donald, step out behind him. Andy goes on about computer camp and chicks and how it's going to be so great, and Donald says his brother says there's a girls' tennis camp right across the lake, then of course Andy digs into Earle about why isn't he running to Harlem to help them poor people. He's sure it's not because he wants to hang out with his friends again. He hasn't even seen them except in school for a fuckin' week. Donald says that speaking of fucking, Earle should see how Kristin, that girl Donald met at Janey's party, makes out. Like she sucks on his tongue for days, but Andy goes, That's all she sucks 'cause she's a prude. Right, Andy, right, Donald says real sarcastically, like Andy's isn't El Barfo. Donald bets Andy can't even get it up for that cow . . . Hey, Earle, where you going? Let's go see *Hand Cannon* at the Quad.

54

Earle, says Janey, who died?

Hello, Janey.

What gives, buddy?

Nothing.

I thought we were becoming friends, she says, watching Earle's eyes. Why don't you come on over to my house, I've got a huge bucketful of my grandma's chocolate-chip cookies.

As the cab jerks, stops, Janey presses Earle's forearm. I've been having some pretty major problems myself, she says. Inside, Earle bumps himself away from her, against the door.

Remember Bill, my boyfriend? I found out he was having this fling with this friend of mine from cheerleading camp; she was at the party. Then, well, I guess you know about me and Mr. Morgan. The whole school knows, I'm sure. Well, when Bill found out, he almost killed me, only I had stopped seeing Mr. Morgan weeks before I met Bill.

Earle studies the New York City Taxi and Limousine Commission's Regulations Regarding Fares In New York City and Its Environs.

Anyway, at least I'm not pregnant anymore. She watches Earle, who watches the street reflections project and pass across his window.

The doorman says, Hello, Janey. The old lady neighbor in the elevator says, Hello, Miss Rosebloom.

You remember where the den is, don't you, Earle, she says, unlocking the front door. I'll get the cookies.

The wall behind the den's bookshelf holds tens of photographs of a balding, smiling man shaking both hands at the same time with Jessica Lange, Joan London, Phoebe Cates, Molly Ringwald, Martha Quinn, Whitney Houston, Jennifer Beals, Cybill Shepherd, Daryl Hannah, Sade, Mary Hart.

Here we go, says Janey as she lands the silver tray of cookies on the pool table. Let me turn on the stereo. Do you like jazz?

Now Earle watches her while Theolonious Monk's "Straight, No Chaser" booms and skitters through the room's six hidden speakers. Janey reaches on tiptoe for the decanter on the bookshelf. Her navy kilt makes it known where her buttocks meet. An old friend of Earle's leans against through cotton the metal teeth of its cage. Janey pours two glasses tall with bourbon.

We both need to get faced, she says.

My girlfriend dumped me. I caught her right in the middle of everything with this guy.

They swallow, and neither coughs. They drink, and drink some more.

Monk still zigzags around the walls, different piano notes peeping out from different corners of the room.

I need to hold somebody, says Janey, laying her arm over his shoulder. Her nose strokes his neck, her lips smear his jugular, her eyelashes brush his jaw. A tear from her touches hot, lengthens quickly to his collarbone, stops, wells again, lengthens quickly under his shirt, over his breast to ball over his nipple. He hugs her, he sweeps his hands over the back of her silk blouse (*sheepsheepsheep*). She kisses his jaw, his chin, his lips; the tip of the tongues lightly touch, lightly touch, swirl over each other. Janey squeezes Earle's chest, then pulls away.

Come on, she says, rising, raising his hand, pulling him up.

She opens the door, and her father's wide bedroom again vibrates brown: mahogany and tortoiseshell and smoked glass. Inside she carefully presses closed the door, she pulls loose the bow around her blouse's neck, she unbuttons it, then dips each shoulder, pulling her arms from the soft holes of silk. She pushes the plaid kilt off her hips, pushes the white slip off her hips, steps from her brown loafers. She reaches behind herself with both hands, unlatches the bra clasp, squeezes her shoulders forward; the bra falls to her elbows, then to the rug. She pushes her white panties off her hips, off her knees; they drop to her toes, she steps free.

She steps toward Earle carefully; his blazer and tie already cover the brown couch. Then he too is nude and she hugs him again, they kiss again. I'm on the pill now. She kisses his dark ear. Both his brown hands replace the white bra, her red nipples grow to warmly stigmatize his palms. He flushes. The sable penis has now risen higher, taps her lily hip. They slow-dance to the bed, kneel together, then lower themselves to the wide support. Rolling on top of him, she rises, her white knees at his colored waist, the vagina at the penis. Earle looks at them, at her creamy breasts, at her face. She smiles. He smiles too. She holds his raven penis, insinuates it into her snowy self. They smile again. Hers is hot and soft; his warm and hard. Her pearl hands pad his inky shoulders; she raises, lowers herself onto, off of him. Her mouth is soon big, her eyes very closed. As her rhythm increases, her thighs flex, relax around him, her white stomach flexes, relaxes too, her wine nipples *are* warm erasers, she *does* moan as he presses her breasts. Cries rise from her mouth but start somewhere much deeper. She now curves back, her fingers squeeze her hair, her elbows high, riding no-handed, cries now short and quick. Then slow.

MmmmmmmmmmmMmmmmm. She rises from him, kisses hard his face, her breasts smear on his chest, her hips and thighs jam the penis, so she lies over him crossways, kisses down the curve of his chin and neck to his clavicle, to each breast; kisses down his stomach, kisses through his pubic hair, returns to kiss his navel. She tilts her head, licks at the penis, at the scrotum, especially the intertesticular area, then licks the underside of the darker ring high on the penis's neck, then the cap itself. She breathes full, eclipses his penis with her mouth. She raises and lowers her face over it, now steadying it with the lips while the tongue presses that darker ring. Earle watches the ceiling as he tugs a bit at her arm, her side, her leg, until she has rotated over him, kneeling. His hands braid over the two small dimples low on her back, then he pulls up to the vagina to press with his pink tongue her pink clitoris, which shines.

Straining between licks, each lap makes the other tighten or curve. Then Janey breathes a long and high cry, twitches quickly.

Now Earle breathes long and high, he freezes, then twitches and pumps. Eventually she raises her mouth from his penis—a moist and even gasket.

I am fully aware that all of you miscreants would rather expend this last day of school listening to Adam Ant or perhaps Beelzebub while snapping your vile bubble gums in my visage, says Mr. Morgan. But I feel it my duty to remind each and every one of you that today is examination day, and if you troglodytes desire to return to this academy in September and if you eventually wish to attend university, I suggest you calm your itchings for the summer respite and behave yourselves. But I would also like to add that it has been both a pleasure and an honor to have been your homeroom advisor this year and to wish each and every one of you nothing but the best in the years to come.

In the front row, Andy and Donald seem ready to race to their computer exam.

mmmMMOOZZ

Donald and Andy sprint to the door; Donald's just enough ahead to check Andy into the wall and slide fast into the computer classroom, like a surfer or something, and of course Andy yells he's got dibs on the Wang, but Donald says that homo, he doesn't, and jumps into the seat first. He bites the Wang, is what Andy says, and Donald says Andy'd love him to.

Earle enters the classroom, and bchind him, Jancy.

Good luck, pal, she says, squeezing his arm.

Commander Considine arrives silently. He writes on the board:

Final Exam: One (1) at least fifty-line program using the gosub function to decipher the following message:

And distributes the following mimeograph to the class:

Sofzs okoysbsr hc o rom og bsk obr og tfsgv og aoao'g vobr-ghofqvsr obr gib-rfwsr dshhwqcoh, o vius, dzowb uofasbh og zofus obr og tfsgv-gaszzwbu og hvs fsjwjoz hsbhg hvoh pzccasr sjsfm giaasf ozcbu Fcihs 49 wb Zckbrsg Qcibhm, Uscfuwo.

It's just a simple frequency distribution program, so it's no sweat. You just have the computer tabulate the frequency of each letter in the text and match that against the frequency distribution of standard written English, then assign each encoded letter its right letter. Like if T appears eighteen point seven percent of the time in the text and F appears eighteen point seven percent of the time in real English, then the F was probably encoded as T. So Trinary all finish in about fifteen minutes and go out to the hall—Earle first, then Andy and Donald tie for second, only of course each one says they beat the other, then Donald tells Earle that their women have this friend, this *exchange* student from *Sweden*. She's great-looking and real tall and blond and has an accent and everything. So what does he say to a little triple-date action tonight to celebrate the last day of school? And Earle says why the hell not.

A very new, soft-blue Cadillac convertible with a clean white roof floats past Earle as he walks home from school. Captain Mee commands the car, smiling.

■ ■

Ironing his pants for tonight's date as he watches *Live at Five* on television, Earle rests the iron upward a moment to grab the underwear on his crotch and squeeze.

Skoal, baby, I'll say to that Swede. Heh, heh.

Today, less than two weeks before the all-important, make-or-break, crucial Democratic primary, announces the model-pretty woman on the show, trying to look stern while her lips luster. And with Al Robinson skyrocketing from the basement dark horse to a virtual dead heat with the heretofore heavily favored shoe-in incumbent, Mayor Feld, here's the most startling news story of the campaign. Nat Mee, a high-ranking member of the Robinson organization and EnnWhyPeeDee precinct captain, in a press conference today charged his own candidate with, quote, "gross misconduct and misappropriation of funds," unquote. Our *Live at Five* Mayoral Race '85 correspondent Raoul García has more . . .

March 10, 1985

Dear Dewayne,

It seems time for us finally to be absolutely honest with each other.

I had no idea I had hurt you so much that you would willfully sabotage your own work (which was proceeding quite nicely, I might add) just to hurt me. Just to hurt my feelings you would have Earle sneak up the stairs, enter Dorothy's apartment without knocking, discover her in a bizarre and (I believe) impossible sexual contortion, then pages later sink to the lowest, most disturbed levels of "scientific" or "biological" pornography this reader has ever had the misfortune to encounter.

I also had no idea that my mistake at the BΛΛ convention would seemingly destroy your faith in black women and in our people as a whole.

The truth is that Richard Johnson and I met at a University

171

of Michigan Writers' Weekend back in '77, and periodically see each other (remember, I do not owe you such a detailed explanation!). As you have probably heard, despite his wealth, fame, and, yes, genius—or perhaps because of it—he is a tremendously lonely man. The attacks on him at the conference for being a "black émigré king divorced from the wants of his people," "a celebrity writer of purely Hebraic angst," hurt him deeply. So Richard needed me. This is not to excuse the hurt I must have caused you, only to explain it.

Throughout the past month I have thought much about our situation. I am fond of you, Dewayne, so have decided *never* to publish my version of your story, to instead sign over all rights to you, then to submit your work myself to my publisher with the highest possible recommendation. I have also decided to accept a reading invitation at Barnard College, Wednesday, May 30. I will arrive that afternoon, lecture from eight to ten o'clock, then will unfortunately have to fly out again the next morning. The college is lodging me at the Sherry Netherlands Hotel.

Whether I am reading too much into your narrative or not, I feel I owe you dinner at Windows on the World. Would you be good enough to escort me there after my lecture? I would like that very much.

So please let us begin our relationship anew. I am sure neither one of us wants to ever again feel it necessary to write phrases like "fucked up the ass like a pig."

Very fondly yours,
Isshee

P.S. A little present:

CHAPTER SEVEN

JUDGMENT DAY

Earle cleaned the corners of his still-sleep-drowsy eyes and looked around Darcelle's clean-smelling room. The soft, small iron bed creaked good morning beneath him. The dresser seemed ancient and worn but still clean and proud. He stepped into his coveralls, opened the door, ready for a new day of learning, and later on, explaining to his mother and sisters yesterday's fight with Bassmouth and Cornbread.

Wail, wail, wail, looka what we got he-are, whined I. Corinthians, his weaselesque countenance shocking Earle's youthful face as the boy entered the room. A belch of the man's gin breath soured Earle's nostrils.

You leave that boy alone, sir, valiantly protested Darcelle, her hands defiantly propped on her strong yet slender hips.

I'm shu-wure his ma'd have a thang or two to say to you hussies if she done knows whut this Pri-ide boy'd been up to in this here cathouse . . . See me and Mister Wyte done know'd 'bout you and yur durn scarlet past even since 'fore you came. You should be 'shamed yo'sef, c'ruptin' a fine young boy like this here.

You are a perverse rodent—ah—Mister Corinthians, isn't it? Terrorizing myself is one matter, barging into my abode early in the morning another, but *never* involve neither my daughter nor her guests, boomed the mother. You may return after the children have had their breakfast if you desire to discuss something with me, she concluded. The skillet in her hands held two tiny lumps of hot grits.

The coward gulped his own sour saliva and stepped back a moment, paralyzed by the righteous fury confronting him. Then he must have remembered that injustice had always been on his side when he said, Ah run this show. You chil'ren run along now. Yo' ma and me gots b'ness.

Dorothy's clenched fists pulsed with furious wrath as she walked out the door—stiffly. Earle followed.

We got school to get to, said Dorothy flatly.

Just then, a brand-new black Hudson turned off Route 49 and slunk toward the home. A middle-aged white man shaped like an egg pushed himself from the driver's seat. As he laboriously walked to the car's trunk, his chins wagged.

That's him! cried Earle. That's him!

That's who?

Why Mister Wyte himself.

The man opened the trunk and extracted something leather, coiled.

C'mon Dorothy. You don't want to watch this.

What? she asked, with terror constricting her voice.

The welcoming ceremony. He usually just saves it fer the menfolk but—

Unseen by the Man, Dorothy bolted behind the house to her mother's bedroom window. Earle ran after.

Dorothy, you can't do nothing. He runs this whole county.

Dorothy said not a word, just watched something vile through the window. Mute.

(*CrackK!*)

Dorothy burst to the front of the house and inside. She snatched up the heavy iron skillet, ran to her mother's bedroom, swung and creased I. Corinthians's leathery head. His eyes turned dead as he released Darcelle's arm, crumpled to the clean hardwood floor.

(*CrackK!*)

Mr. Wyte, his pants at his knees, his pathetic pink pud nearly clothed by flaps of fat, lashed the whip again—*crackK!*—his long wish-fulfillment slashing black, cutting Dorothy's arm. The skillet clattered to the floor, mashing dead Corinthians's ugly nose.

Ah'll take care of you aftuh ah take care of yo' ma, hissed the pig.

At that, Darcelle's heretofore empty eyes ignited with tremendous maternal wrath. Proudly bare-chested, she boomed, If you touch my girl, I shall kill you dead.

The fat man looked up at the hand-hewn ceiling and laughed and laughed—then approached young Dorothy, stuffing the doorway with his weight, his already stubby stride reduced to a mere waddle by the shackles of his crumpled pants and soiled shorts. As he clawed the young woman's shoulders, Darcelle, the mother, sped her leg from behind to meet his bantam sex. Wyte screamed, folded over his wound, but before the two women could race out the door—*crackK!*—he stung Darcelle in her cleft magic. Now she too screamed as Mr. Wyte approached mechanically. Suddenly Wyte straightened, opened wide his mouth and his eyes, then slumped onto Corinthians's corpse. Where that terror had just stood so menacingly, Earle now appeared, a red-stained kitchen knife in his hand. He threw it to a corner (*clatterclatterclatter*).

After weeks of night traveling and half-truths, the three joined the migrant farmworker circuit, picking cotton in Arkansas, Louisiana, and Texas, chilies in Arizona, then in California tomatoes, lettuce, and finally artichokes in Monterey. They worked while there was light, every day, were paid almost enough to feed themselves as they traveled; yet at least in their grueling, nomadic existence no one asked questions. Their past was their own.

In Monterey, California, Darcelle finally found a job waitressing that paid enough to let the children go to school again. Until then Darcelle had relied upon her own aborted college education to educate her flamebearers. For the outside world, Earle and Dorothy called each other "brother" and "sister" but the unbreakable, unshatterable cord that so wonderfully wrapped them together was hardly sororal or fraternal. So one summer's day, on a stretch of Northern Californian beach known only to them, lying on their backs counting clouds, Earle began to cry.

My family, my mama, he sobbed.

Dorothy held his hand, then kissed his tears. Earle smiled weakly and kissed her back. Their lips now pressed together, still neither one had yet realized why such a simple, innocent touch had so fired their very souls.

Silently they kissed on, smoothing hands over sensitive swells that swelled still more under every soft touch. Now naked before the surf's mighty shout, they made love, not knowing how "technically" yet succeeding so triumphantly, so very gloriously, because it finally allowed them to release their raging adolescent emotions. Yes, their lovemaking was what all good lovemaking always is—a wordless "I love you."

Long after the War, when they were married and both schoolteachers and the children were with their grandmother, the two would giddily return to their private stretch of coastline, saying "I love you" again and again in that very same special way.

The
End

[Much applause.] I had planned on reading yet another selection from *Hog Jowl Junction,* but it seems that time does not permit if I am going to answer some of your questions . . . Yes, the young woman in blue.

Q: How many hours a day do you write?

A: Well, there are those tiresome, fuddy-duddy authors who will tell you, "You must write every day four hours a day, seven days a week, rain or shine," as if only in this way can you write well; as if only through tremendous hard work and dinotherian dedication can you ever even hope to succeed . . . Those writers are absolutely right [the audience mumbles happy laughter]. But to answer your question, I write four hours a day, seven days a week, rain or shine. [More laughter, then Isshee nods at a pale young woman in black, with round glasses and spirited hair.]

Q: I know you get asked this all the time but—

A: Baldwin, Hughes, Johnson of course, Walker, Morrison, Wolfe, Eliot, Fitzgerald, and lately I have begun reading some postmodern works that are much better than I would have once thought . . . Does that answer your question?

[The blushing and smiling questioner nods. There is much laughter. A woman in a plaid workshirt speaks.]

Q: You have been criticized by some, I might say blatantly sexist, critics, for being anti-male. What do you have to say to their kind?

A: I think to a large degree they are correct, especially in my very early works. I began writing shortly after some rather disastrous romantic encounters, one with a university professor no less, and my early works reflected this misandry. However, a male author can write five hundred pages about women who are either prostitutes and therefore, in his eyes, honest, or Jezebels who do nothing but break hearts, marry men for money, and are pathologically unfaithful. These writers are the norm and rarely labeled "anti-female." [wild applause]

The heroine is almost nonexistent in literature *and* film. In fact, it is unusual in either a spy novel or, let's say, an adventure movie to have more than two women in the entire work. We need only remember *Star Wars* with its cast of literally thousands but only two women—a sweethearted aunt who is soon killed and a princess. And it is this princess who is supposedly the offering to appease we feminists. Her type is the "tough-but-beautiful broad," more stout of character than even the men in the film!—except, of course, than the hero, and the arch-villain who captures her and forces her to wear scanty clothing until the hero saves her and finally bestows upon her that magical macho kiss that makes her abandon her career as, oh, perhaps, a world-renowned archaeologist, to spend the remainder of her days polishing *his* pith helmet. [laughter/whistling/applause]

So perhaps society can withstand even a little more male-as-bad-guy literature, but we certainly cannot afford any more anti-female works. [More applause, then she speaks in an overly deep voice.] . . . And I promise, elected . . . [laughter] . . . Next quest—Oh, Professor Drake is pulling her index finger across her neck. I guess that means we're out of time. Yes, now she's nodding, so I am *sure* that is what she was trying to non-verbally communicate. [Isshee chuckles with the audience.] Well, thank you all very much, and good night. [More applause; then one, then many, then all stand and applaud.]

Isshee twists her wrist, looks at her watch, lays her books and notes in her soft straw bag, runs down the stage stairs—without looking—into

Oh—

Excuse—

Me—

Excuse *me,* says Dewayne. Hello.

Mister Wellington, I'm glad you made it.

A standing ovation. I am very impressed.

Oh, it always happens at these women's colleges. [laughs] Would you still care to accept my invitation to Windows on the World?

Actually, I was thinking of Picaresque, it's much closer.

And more fitting, I suppose. Or perhaps Chic? then dancing at Spazio?

Luckily, they don't exist. Not yet anyway. [laughs]

Dewayne waves at a cab on Broadway. It stops in the center of the street, across both lanes. He quickly opens the door, she, then he, squat inside.

I was under the impression that cabs do not stop for we Afro-Americans uptown.

They don't *going* uptown, into Harlem. But we're going downtown to the Upper West Side. Where de rich folks live at.

But you live there too.

Courtesy of my ex-wife.

Ah yes, I remember.

Nonsense! she says. I shall pay—or rather, Barnard College. She passes the black driver $5 for the $2.50 clicked on the meter. Outside the cab she explains that she always tries to redistribute the wealth when someone else is paying.

Here it is, she says, *rosy, marbled columns and brass track lighting and hanging plants under the neon cursive* Picaresque.

I am flattered by your memory. He ceremoniously swings back the mahogany and smoked-glass door.

Isshee smiles largely as the handsome, Lebanese-looking man approaches, his arms forward and upturned.

You must be Yassir. Good evening.

Hussein stops and watches Isshee oddly. *Sorry?* he says. Two tonight, Mr. Wellington?

Isshee whispers to Dewayne, I am so embarrassed, I could kill you. They sit.

My name is Shawn, I'll be your food server for this evening, says Shawn, this evening's food server.

Your dessert menu for the lady, please. Isshee watches Dewayne a bit after the word *lady*. But I will have your Black Forest Cake and a cappuccino.

Well, begins Shawn, we have Creamy Chocolate Torte Deluxe, that's a fresh-baked torte crust filled with creamed milk chocolate similar to a truffle filling, with finely chopped hazelnuts mixed in, all topped with fresh dairy whipped cream and Bulgarian bitter-chocolate shavings. Black Forest Cake, which you are already familiar with—

French-fried chocolate ice cream? she asks slowly.

Of course. Something to drink?

A cappuccino for me also. She watches Dewayne. Stop smiling.

Since you've finished your contribution to *Platitudes*, Isshee— which I enjoyed and of course appreciated—what are you working on now?

I am critiquing—um—Johnson's *Far, So Very Far from Home* for the *Times;* then after a brief vacation I am toying with the idea of writing the screenplay for *My Big Ol' Feets Gon' Stomp Dat Evil Down*. Universal took out an option on it years ago . . . I realize that screenwriters are absolutely the lowest form of writer, yet, I must confess, the salaries paid are—as they say—staggering. Naturally I am also interested in writing my own script to ensure no situation-comedy hack mutilates it . . . But you, Dewayne. What are your plans after finishing the book?

Actually, I would like to sell *Platitudes* to Hollywood and, with the money, build a cottage in a secluded section of Martha's Vineyard, where I have some property. My goal is no longer to have to depend upon alimony for my subsistence.

Ah ha, so you should be grateful to we feminists. Before the Women's Rights movement, no man would *ever* have received alimony from his wife.

The food and drinks are eaten and drunk. After the waiter asks, Will that be all? Dewayne says, Yes, thank you. Isshee again pays the bill.

A cab stops under Isshee's raised hand.

Before you go, if you would like to see my den, where I work, where it all comes from, I would be delighted to show you. I live nearby.

Excuse me, sir, Isshee says to the Haitian cabbie, handing him a dollar. Never mind.

They walk to Ninetieth Street and West End Avenue without words. Isshee watches the buildings as they pass.

This must be yours, because there are *St. Rita's School for Girls' imposing and ornate Gothic gates* across the street. You are right. You never *do* know when this kind of structure will pop up. [laughs]

Jerry the doorman opens the door for the two, says good night.

Have a seat in the living room, I'll be right back. Coltrane's "My Favorite Things" is still pinned on the turntable. He pushes Start. In the kitchen, he fills a carafe with Pinot Grigio, pulls out from the freezer two frosted wineglasses, careful to touch only the stems.

In the living room, to the right of the statue of a Haitian woman going to market, to the left of the wall Pollocked with many-colored overlapping splashes, Dewayne lands the tray on the coffee table covered with Ghanaian Kinte cloth.

Pinot Grigio, she says after a sip. I am duly impressed. Both on the couch, Dewayne turns to her; she rises and looks through the wooden slat shades. Ah yes, I remember you saying you faced Broadway.

My den's over he—

Ah ha! Fifi LaGrande's Académie Américaine, I knew it! You changed the name of the ballet studio to Signora Montovani's because the French sounded contrived. Perhaps also to avoid prosecution, hmm?

Here, in here is where I work.

On his desk, notebooks and pens cross, cover each other. A typewriter lies on the floor. A hand-drawn map of the neighborhood dangles from a too long, ripped rectangle of tape from the window.

And Saint Rita's outside this window. I do not even have to look. I feel as if I am backstage at a magic act. I also feel we are supposed to make love.

They near each other slowly, they kiss so lightly—with just the tips of their lips.

I . . . I . . . he says.

They kiss again, this time while walking to the bedroom. They unbutton, unzip, push down and push off each other's clothes; kiss and stroke. She softly pushes away from him, lips last. She lifts her straw bag from the floor. Naked, she walks to the bathroom.

Dewayne spits on, strokes, then yanks at his semi-hard penis.

Isshee returns smiling, lies on him. They kiss more, caress. She reaches past his navel.

How'd you like to take a nap or something? says Dewayne. I'll wake you when it's ready. I'm sorry. It's been quite a long while.

She kisses him again, smiles, lays her head on his chest, and sleeps.

He looks down at, lifts up, his penis, holds it, frees it; again it slouches.

After watching the ceiling and the stereo's green glowing dials, and sliding his hand from her soft, soft back and over the soft wide curve of her hip and buttock and back again, he slowly, slowly, turns himself from under her. He walks slowly and naked to the den.

58

Now seven-thirty, Earle has another free hour before meeting Sonja the Swede.

MMMoozzz.

Hello, Earle. Bet you're surprised to see me.

He does not speak.

I did what I did, Earle, because I wanted to. Because Richard is very sexy, because I care about you differently; I care about you *too much* whether you believe that or not. You're too pure. And sometimes I didn't need pure; I didn't have time all the time for pure and ice skating and Coney Island because I am not that way. . . . Who wanted to fall in love with a fat nerd.

He is choking, trying to swallow his tears, then shakily, convulsively he breathes out and cries and cries one continuous siren and she cries too and they hold each other, lock each other with their arms, their tears wetting each other's cheeks. Now her kisses the warmth on his neck, a warmth that rises to his jaw and chin and he kisses her lips which are salt-watered and again and again he kisses short to prove he can, kisses her cheeks to her eyes down to her nose to her lips again, he can, and she kisses back too, *just* as much, and then he's aware that his heart's crazily banging because it's never felt this before, no fire drill, the real thing, and he wonders how he had ever lived so long without it.

Now that it presses the underside of his desk, he will go wake Isshee.

For my mom and dad,
wish you were here.

About the Author

Trey Ellis was born in Washington, D.C., in 1962. He attended Phillips Academy, Andover, and Stanford University, where he was the editor of his college humor magazine, *The Stanford Chaparral*. He has worked in Italy as a translator and has traveled extensively throughout Africa and Central America. Mr. Ellis's journalistic work has appeared in *The Black Film Review, Art & Antiques, Newsweek, Elle, Interview,* and *The Washington Post. Platitudes* is his first novel, and he lives in New York.

VINTAGE
CONTEMPORARIES

___	**Love Always** by Ann Beattie	$5.95	394-74418-7
___	**First Love and Other Sorrows** by Harold Brodkey	$5.95	679-72075-8
___	**The Debut** by Anita Brookner	$5.95	394-72856-4
___	**Cathedral** by Raymond Carver	$4.95	394-71281-1
___	**Bop** by Maxine Chernoff	$5.95	394-75522-7
___	**I Look Divine** by Christopher Coe	$5.95	394-75995-8
___	**Dancing Bear** by James Crumley	$5.95	394-72576-X
___	**The Last Good Kiss** by James Crumley	$6.95	394-75989-3
___	**One to Count Cadence** by James Crumley	$5.95	394-73559-5
___	**The Wrong Case** by James Crumley	$5.95	394-73558-7
___	**The Last Election** by Pete Davies	$6.95	394-74702-X
___	**A Narrow Time** by Michael Downing	$6.95	394-75568-5
___	**From Rockaway** by Jill Eisenstadt	$6.95	394-75761-0
___	**Platitudes** by Trey Ellis	$6.95	394-75439-5
___	**Days Between Stations** by Steve Erickson	$6.95	394-74685-6
___	**Rubicon Beach** by Steve Erickson	$6.95	394-75513-8
___	**A Fan's Notes** by Frederick Exley	$7.95	679-72076-6
___	**Pages from a Cold Island** by Frederick Exley	$6.95	394-75977-X
___	**A Piece of My Heart** by Richard Ford	$5.95	394-72914-5
___	**Rock Springs** by Richard Ford	$6.95	394-75700-9
___	**The Sportswriter** by Richard Ford	$6.95	394-74325-3
___	**The Ultimate Good Luck** by Richard Ford	$5.95	394-75089-6
___	**Fat City** by Leonard Gardner	$5.95	394-74316-4
___	**Ellen Foster** by Kaye Gibbons	$5.95	394-75757-2
___	**Within Normal Limits** by Todd Grimson	$5.95	394-74617-1
___	**Airships** by Barry Hannah	$5.95	394-72913-7
___	**Dancing in the Dark** by Janet Hobhouse	$5.95	394-72588-3
___	**November** by Janet Hobhouse	$6.95	394-74665-1
___	**Saigon, Illinois** by Paul Hoover	$6.95	394-75849-8
___	**Fiskadoro** by Denis Johnson	$5.95	394-74367-9
___	**The Stars at Noon** by Denis Johnson	$5.95	394-75427-1
___	**Asa, as I Knew Him** by Susanna Kaysen	$4.95	394-74985-5
___	**Lulu Incognito** by Raymond Kennedy	$6.95	394-75641-X
___	**Steps** by Jerzy Kosinski	$5.95	394-75716-5
___	**A Handbook for Visitors From Outer Space** by Kathryn Kramer	$5.95	394-72989-7
___	**The Chosen Place, the Timeless People** by Paule Marshall	$6.95	394-72633-2
___	**Suttree** by Cormac McCarthy	$6.95	394-74145-5
___	**The Bushwhacked Piano** by Thomas McGuane	$5.95	394-72642-1
___	**Nobody's Angel** by Thomas McGuane	$6.95	394-74738-0
___	**Something to Be Desired** by Thomas McGuane	$4.95	394-73156-5
___	**To Skin a Cat** by Thomas McGuane	$5.95	394-75521-9
___	**Bright Lights, Big City** by Jay McInerney	$5.95	394-72641-3
___	**Ransom** by Jay McInerney	$5.95	394-74118-8
___	**The All-Girl Football Team** by Lewis Nordan	$5.95	394-75701-7
___	**River Dogs** by Robert Olmstead	$6.95	394-74684-8

V I N T A G E
CONTEMPORARIES

___ **Soft Water** by Robert Olmstead	$6.95	394-75752-1
___ **Family Resemblances** by Lowry Pei	$6.95	394-75528-6
___ **Norwood** by Charles Portis	$5.95	394-72931-5
___ **Clea & Zeus Divorce** by Emily Prager	$6.95	394-75591-X
___ **A Visit From the Footbinder** by Emily Prager	$6.95	394-75592-8
___ **Mohawk** by Richard Russo	$6.95	394-74409-8
___ **Anywhere But Here** by Mona Simpson	$6.95	394-75559-6
___ **Carnival for the Gods** by Gladys Swan	$6.95	394-74330-X
___ **Myra Breckinridge and Myron** by Gore Vidal	$8.95	394-75444-1
___ **The Car Thief** by Theodore Weesner	$6.95	394-74097-1
___ **Breaking and Entering** by Joy Williams	$6.95	394-75773-4
___ **Taking Care** by Joy Williams	$5.95	394-72912-9

On sale at bookstores everywhere, but if otherwise unavailable, may be ordered from us. You can use this coupon, or phone (800) 638-6460.

Please send me the Vintage Contemporaries books I have checked on the reverse. I am enclosing $_____ (add $1.00 per copy to cover postage and handling). Send check or money order—no cash or CODs, please. Prices are subject to change without notice.

NAME _____

ADDRESS _____

CITY_____ STATE _____ ZIP _____

Send coupons to:
RANDOM HOUSE, INC., 400 Hahn Road, Westminster, MD 21157
ATTN: ORDER ENTRY DEPARTMENT
Allow at least 4 weeks for delivery.